THE CHLOE FILES

My name is Chloe Everson. I'm a dancer at the Red Lagoon in New Salem, Maine. The things I'm going to tell you may seem impossible, unreal, but they're true. I've seen them with my own eyes. All I can say is be careful...there's evil out there...waiting...

ASHES TO ASHES

A silver locket said to have belonged to Joan of Arc and a children's nursery rhyme...

A 600-year-old monkey with an attitude and a mysterious supernatural symbol on a Caller ID box...

A deadly plague reemerging in the seaside town of New Salem, Maine, and the manifestation of a little girl's ghost...

How do these tie in with the sudden disappearance of Chloe's fiancé, Detective Sergeant Arlo Grimm, while on a routine search for a lead to her twin sister, who vanished thirty years earlier?

When the answer points to an Evil she'd thought vanquished Chloe knows she's in over her pretty blonde head and this time she'll have nothing to rely on except her own wits and courage.

But will that be enough to save her and the life of the man she loves?

THE CHLOE FILES #1: ASHES TO ASHES
by Howard Hopkins

First print and electronic editions: March, 2008

Copyright © 2007, 2008 by Howard Hopkins
www.howardhopkins.com

Cover by Howard Hopkins

ISBN 978-0-6151-9452-3

Published by Golden Perils Press
www.lulu.com/goldenperils
Email: goldenperils@aol.com

Printed in the United States of America

THE
CHLOE FILES

#1: ASHES TO ASHES

by

Howard Hopkins

ONE

Where in the World is Arlo Grimm?

I need help.

Wait, I should back up a little and introduce myself before I start telling my story. Arly always says I'm too impetuous.

My name is Chloe Everson. I'm blonde, 5'6" and, um, thirty-something. Oh, and please don't judge me, but I'm also a stripper at the Red Lagoon, at least I was until a few weeks ago before...well, that's a story I can get into later. Most of the other girls call themselves exotic dancers, like it makes taking off your clothes in front of a bunch of drunken idiots classier somehow. But I am a stripper. There's an art to it, like those burlesque girls in the old days.

I never had a lot of control over what happened in my life. In fact, most of the time I just felt like everything was sweeping me along in a rush of black water. But stripping gives me some sense of control. I know exactly what I am doing and what I can make my audience do. Anyone who gets out of line, well, Arly takes care of them.

And I know what you're thinking: I'm one of "those" girls. Well, I'm not. It goes no farther than the dancing and never has. I have never crossed that line and I wouldn't. I just spend a lot of time naked and I don't mind that. Guys don't seem to mind, either, but it's strictly look, don't touch.

I hope what I've told you won't make you think less of me. I ended up on my own early, and had to survive somehow. I had no real skills other than dancing and I made enough money to give me some sense of power over the things in my life I might not have had otherwise.

I've been through a lot over the past few months, especially back around Christmas when that whole Sisters of the Snake thing was go-

ing on. You can read about that in GRIMM. It's now a matter of re-
cord since Arly decided to hire that author to report the things we've
seen and experienced. I mean, who would believe it if we didn't make
sure the public was able to read about it? Arly didn't even believe in
the supernatural before Angelique Ficatier and her witches came into
our lives.

Me, I just write things down in my journal. I'm doing that now, sitting here in my condo, with the boxes I've packed piled all around me
(I had plans, you know, ones that now...) I was hoping maybe someday
I would be able to show it to my children, let them see what a fire-
cracker their mother was in her day. Sounds silly, doesn't it? Like one
of those old movies I like to watch. The kind where the heroes always
win and the guy gets the girl and everything turns out happily ever after.

But life is not always like that and I'm afraid maybe this time I've
lost again, lost someone who means more to me than anything in the
world. I've lost a lot in my life. My parents were killed when I was
seven and I was sent to various foster homes. My sister...I lost her, too.
I haven't been able to find her since the day I saw a couple drive off
with her and leave me behind. Arly was helping me look for her, but I
already tried everything I could think of. Still, I cling to a little hope
that someday...

Well, anyway, I guess that's enough about me for now, because
what's more important is that I am worried. Sorry, no, I'm not just
worried. I'm scared out of my wits. Because after what happened with
the Sisters of the Snake I know there are things in this world that crawl
out of the darkness and into our lives. Terrible things. Inhuman things.
And I'm afraid something like that has happened again. To Arly.

He disappeared about a week ago. I've been looking everywhere,
trying everything I could think of. But I'm not the detective. Arly is.
He's the one who knows how to find people. I talked to his friend, Detective Sturdevant, about it and he's helping but hasn't come up with
any leads yet. I can tell he's worried too, because before Angelique
Ficatier he didn't believe in any of that ghost and demon stuff, either. I
think he does now, but he's afraid to admit it. I can't say I blame him.

Oh, dammit, it's starting to rain. I can see the water streaking down
the slider doors that lead to the patio. I hate rain. It just makes everything more depressing right now. Makes me more afraid and more

lonely and I feel like I'm just going to come apart if I don't do something, find some clue to what happened to him.

Even though it's raining I am thinking of driving over to Arly's cottage to look around. I've been there already a few times and found nothing, but just being in his house makes me feel a little bit closer to him, so maybe I'll try again.

What else can I do?

TWO

Squirrels and Monkeys

2:45am...

It's raining squirrels and monkeys.

I remember my dad saying that to me when I was little. He thought it was funny. I guess at five or six years old I did, too. I remember giggling, anyway. And take my word for it, that didn't happen a lot after I lost them.

Squirrels and monkeys. That was my dad. Simple cats and dogs weren't good enough for his little girls. Everything had to be special.

As you might have guessed I can't sleep. That's why I am bundled up on the couch in the darkness of my condo's sunken living room, staring out through the slider doors. The rain was pouring down. Squirrels and monkeys.

I was trying to read, a horror book called *Night Demons* by that author I told you about, the one writing down Arly's cases for him, Howard Hopkins. The book is good enough but I had a hard time focusing on it and the subject matter...well, maybe horror's not the best thing for me right now. Because fiction can't come close to the real supernatural things Arly and I seem to attract.

Doesn't matter, anyway, because the power took a powder with the last crash of thunder a few minutes ago. So did most of my composure.

I never used to be afraid of the dark. But since Ficatier and her Sisters and my coma...the dark hides things. Parents tell their children there's nothing to be frightened of in the dark, but they're wrong. There's plenty to be scared of.

You might also guess I decided not to go over to Arly's cottage to-night. With the rain and my mood I thought I might break down if I went there. I should be stronger, right? I've faced things others never dreamed existed. And in many ways I *am* stronger for it. In other ways...not so much.

But I have limits. Like I've said, I've been through a lot in my life and even if I am not exactly sure what those limits are, I am sure I've gotten too close to them as of late.

Lightning suddenly turned my living room into a canvas of vanilla and shadow. A boom followed it three seconds later—one-thousand-one, one-thousand-two, one-thousand-three—that's how my dad always taught me to count the lightning's distance and three seconds between the flash and the crash meant it was three miles away. Not sure whether that's true, but it was too damn close and the crash launched me off the couch. The *Night Demons* book and the throw blanket ended up on the floor and I'm not about to bother feeling around in the dark for them.

I bumped my shin on the frickin' coffee table, too. That felt good. I said a word Arly probably wouldn't have liked, but sometimes I have a mouth.

I took a couple deep breaths, then reached down and grabbed my cup of decaf. It was cold now, and didn't help my nerves much. I think some of it spilled when I banged into the table, because the cup slid around when I put it back down.

The rain suddenly came down harder, pouring and roaring. Squirrels and monkeys. The thought brought no giggle this time, only more loneliness over missing my folks and Arly, and helplessness over not knowing what to do next.

Dammit, this wasn't me. I wasn't helpless. If not for me the Sisters of the Snake would have killed Arly at the D.A.'s mansion. There has to be something I can do. I just need to stop feeling sorry for myself and imagining the worst. I've taken care of myself just fine for years and coming apart now won't help.

Arms wrapped about myself, I drifted over to the slider doors. The woods beyond the condo were just a black mass distorted by the water streaking down the glass. At least there were no zombies lurking on the patio this time (hey, it happened not so long ago, so don't get the idea I'm paranoid or crazy).

I giggled. Maybe it was more from nerves than anything else, but I got no time to think about it because lightning glazed the dark clouds and washed across the patio.

And something jumped at the glass! I let out one of those bleats that come reflexively when a mouse runs across your bare feet.

Oh, crap, I think I might have just peed in my nightgown...

THREE

Monkey Business

I was lucky. I didn't pee in my nightgown, but it sure as hell felt like I had, because everything below my waist went cold. I thought I might actually collapse there for a second, but I kept telling myself: I've been through worse...I've been through worse...I've been through worse...I was just startled. That's all.

Why was I startled?

Because there are things you don't expect to see on your patio in Maine. Zombies are one of them, though in New Salem that's happened to me. (You can read all about Chuckles and my patio in GRIMM because I don't want to relive that nightmare right now when I am so scared I think I just might really piss myself.)

Anyway, other than me or Arly, most people wouldn't expect to find certain things like zombies on their patio.

Monkeys, either.

We don't have monkeys in Maine, at least not running around free on rained-drenched nights. But I swear what jumped at the window was a monkey. A monkey with a little skull face!

I shivered and everything jiggled, but not in a good way. I squeezed my arms about myself so tight I started to lose all feeling in my hands.

Lightning flashed again and I jumped.

And saw the monkey. Only this time he had a regular monkey face, not a little skull, and he was doing that weird monkey thing with his scalp—you know, instant monkey face lift. It looked like one of those little Capuchin monkeys. They always have this look on their faces like they're passing a kidney stone.

Thunder crashed and I couldn't stop another one of those bleats from escaping my lips. It was made worse because that damn monkey let out a screech, too.

Like my nerves weren't already jangled enough.

It's times like this, when I'm scared enough to cough up my pounding heart, I remember the stupidest things. Like how monkeys creep me out.

Well, maybe that's not so stupid because there's a damn monkey on my patio and I have no idea where the hell it might have come from or what it's doing there. But a memory from when I was little, before my parents died, invaded my panicked mind. They had taken me and Patricia—Patricia's my twin sister, the one I've never been able to find—to York Animal Farm. It wasn't really a farm, more an amusement park with a zoo where you could feed goats and sheep and pet other animals, the ones not likely to bite your hand off.

There were monkey cages. Monkeys do some strange things. They're like half-witted little old men who think peeing on a public wall is funny for some strange reason. They have some weird habits. Some of those habits...

There was this one monkey my sister thought was cute. A moment after this little reprobate flung a handful of poop that hit her smack in the face the cuteness wore off.

I thought it was funny at the time, until the monkey grabbed the bars and started jerking himself back and forth and peeling his monkey lips back from his teeth like he thought the whole thing was an insane joke.

That's when I somehow concluded the monkey wasn't laughing. He was psychotic and getting even for being in the cage and letting the human beings gawking at him know he wasn't going to take their crap anymore.

What can I say? I was a kid. It was a weird thing to think but nobody ever really accused me of being all that normal. From that point on the little buggers have creeped me out.

A tapping on the slider door pulled me out of the memory and I tried to see the monkey in the darkness. My eyes had adjusted pretty well since the lightning flash and I could make out the fact the monkey had something in his hand and was tapping it against the window.

I hoped it wasn't poop.

FOUR

Ring-a-Ring

You'll probably think I'm stupid and you might be right.

You know how the idiot girl in all those bad horror movies goes down in the cellar or up the darkened stairs when she just knows a psychotic killer's lurking about the place? I'm always yelling at them for that—well, I yell at the screen and Arly sinks into his seat, embarrassed, but that's beside the point—but getting a small hold on my composure I knelt in front of the slider door and pulled the pipe from the track, the one I use to stop the door from opening because Arly told me a lot of robbers get in that way. I kept hold of it in case the monkey jumped at me when I slid the door back. I love animals but creepy little monkeys whose faces look like skulls even for a second are in another ballpark and if that little sucker attacked me I fully intended to brain him.

I noticed my hand shaking a little as I reached up for the slider lock and eased it down. The click it made sounded abnormally loud even against the rain beating down outside and made me bite my tongue. That hurt.

But it was nothing compared to the startled bleat that came out of my mouth a second later.

Yeah, OK, another one of those mouse-skittering-across-your-toes bleats. I do that a lot so maybe you should just get used to it. I've always had a hair-trigger startle response, even more so since the Sisters of the Snake did what they did to me.

All I know is a second later the pipe flew out of my hand and landed on the carpet a half-dozen feet away and I went backward to land smack on my ass. I'm usually glad I have a lot of padding there but I hit my tailbone and it hurt worse than biting my tongue.

I tried to swallow my heart, which was thudding in my throat, and again found myself struggling not to pee myself.

It took me a stunned moment to realize what had caused my fright and I felt more than a little foolish, because if I had seen it in a movie I would have laughed.

The phone was ringing. That's all it was.

I forced myself to breathe and the monkey tapped on the window again, scaring the crap out of me. If the pipe had still been in my hand I would have thrown it through the glass at him.

The phone kept ringing and it dawned on me it was now past three in the morning and nobody would be calling unless it was...

Bad news. It was always bad news when the phone rang late at night.

Shaking, I got to my feet, ignoring the tapping monkey for the time being. I went to the end table and grabbed the phone, noticing the caller ID was flashing.

But that was impossible. The phone still rang when the power went out but the caller ID couldn't work—I still had one of the separate arrangements on this phone for emergency situations if the power was out.

No number came up, though. Just a weird, three-transomed, multi-angled symbol of some sort that kept tracking across the small green back-lit screen. I didn't recognize it.

The phone jangled again and I grabbed it, my heart back in my throat.

"Arly?" I blurted, almost afraid of the response.

A sound came from the other end, a distorted faltering thing. Like a garbled transmission, overlaid with white noise.

*Chloe...*a voice came from the other end, with a searing edge, and as if coming from some great distance.

It wasn't Arly. It wasn't even male.

"Who is this?"

Chloe...

The voice was female, young, I'm pretty sure, but it was so distorted it was hard to tell. One thing I was sure about, it said my name and carried a familiarity that made my small hairs tingle like a bunch of ants doing the wild thing on the back of my neck. I felt horribly cold all over.

"Please, who is this? What do you want?" Why is it we can only think of saying something obvious when we're the most scared? And why is it we ascribe the most catastrophic scenarios to what might be perfectly innocuous, like a bad phone connection?

That's how I suddenly felt, as if the worst doom I could imagine was on the other end of the line and the Devil was calling to tell me about it.

You're being silly, I assured myself. It didn't help. It never does, no matter how many self-help books you read.

Ring...ring-a-ring of roses...a pocket full of posies...ashes, ashes...

If I thought I was cold before I now felt like I had fallen off the Titanic.

Because I suddenly knew why the voice sounded familiar.

"Patricia?" I said, half a whisper. No, it wasn't possible.

But I remember...I remember when we were kids, before the foster home split us up and I lost her, we would play that silly child's game. It was one of the few light moments we had after our parents' deaths, and I recall her face, a smiling reflection of my own.

*We...all...fall...down...*her voice came again, startling me from my memory.

It wasn't possible. Even if after all these years Patricia had somehow found me, my twin sister would be the same age and this was a little girl's voice.

The phone line went dead with a boom of thunder and I swore my heart stopped, then jumped into my mouth. I dropped the phone and the dial tone mocked me. Lightning momentarily illuminated the room and everything seemed somehow alien and threatening, but that part, at least, was only my imagination.

What wasn't my imagination or a product of my own dread was the sudden burst of chilled air that washed across the back of my nightgown.

I'd like to say I let out another of those mouse-across-the-toes bleats but I couldn't even get out a sound.

Because when I turned the slider door was open a foot and still moving...

FIVE

Ding Dong the Monkey's Gone

The monkey had gotten tired of waiting for me to open the door, because when I turned he had his little monkey hand clamped about its edge and was forcing it back. I concluded two things right there: A) monkeys were stronger than I had given them credit for and, B) if he jumped at me, no matter how strong he was, I was going to kick some monkey ass.

That is, if I could get over being frozen where I stood.

The monkey pushed the door open another foot. I glanced to my right, hoping to see where the pipe had landed but it was too dark. I could barely see the monkey in the ambient light bleeding in from beyond the slider door.

A burst of chilled moist wind slapped at my nightgown and when I looked back Curious Skullface had sashayed into my living room. A flash of lightning startled me out of my paralysis. The monkey peered at me, his forehead doing that weird jerky monkey thing, but at least the monkey skull face didn't come back. He made some kind of clicky chirping noise and that didn't help my nerves in the least.

"Get out of here!" I yelled at him. "Go on—shoo!" Pretty brave, huh? I mean, I'd faced cult killers and sorceresses with Arly and here I was about to pee my nightgown over an organ grinder's reject.

Monkeys bite, don't they? What if he had rabies or something? *Don't be silly!* I told myself. He wasn't charging or drooling. I was just making up excuses for being such a wuss.

The monkey walked forward a few steps. Well, he didn't really walk, he sort of loped, holding out his hand, as if offering something.

Last time I saw anything like that Pat got poop in the face and I wasn't in any mood for that.

He made more monkey sounds. In shadow, he set whatever was in his hand on the carpet, uttered a squeak, then whirled and scurried to the slider. He bolted through the door and let me tell you I was frickin' glad he was gone. And glad I was monkey poopless.

A shudder made my teeth clack together and I gulped a deep breath. Then I ran to the slider and yanked it shut. It took me a minute, still shaking, to locate the damn pipe and jam it back in the track.

"Jeez!" I blurted, shuddering a last time. It was my own fault. I had pulled the pipe out in the first place and unlocked the door. Whether that was courage or stupidity I wasn't going to argue, though I was inclined to accept the latter.

Arly would have said curiosity. If people thought cats were curious...well, Chloes were even more so and I had to admit he was right. I had a habit of charging into things without thinking on them for too long, no matter how scared I was. And though one little monkey wasn't as likely to kill me as a few three-hundred-year-old witches, I still should have been more careful. Because Arly was missing and wasn't around to get me out of trouble. This time it was my turn to get him out of it.

I suddenly remembered the monkey had left something on my rug and reminded myself to watch where I stepped, just in case. I didn't imagine getting monkey poop out of the carpet would be any joy.

I reached monkey ground zero and knelt, goosebumps tingling all over my skin. It was too dark to see the object until another flash of lightning revealed it wasn't monkey droppings.

I reached for it...

SIX

Morning Comes on Monkey Feet

6:47am...

I woke up on the couch, my fingers clamped to the pipe from the slider. I had decided the odds of a robber breaking in that way were far less than odds of me braining anybody who even tried to sneak up on me after the monkey left.

It was one of those annoyingly bright mornings that happen here in New Salem after a night of thunderstorms. I tried prying my eyes open, but the glare stung like needles, so I pressed my lids shut for another few minutes. A low-grade headache throbbed in the back of my neck from the awkward position I had slept in and some of the fear from the night remained. My mouth tasted like a cat had slept in it—no, make that a monkey. A little creepy monkey with a sometimes skull face who'd deposited something on my carpet I was sure was going to turn out to be a whole lot more problematic than monkey poop.

A few minutes later I finally managed to get my eyes to stay open at half-mast with only a minimum amount of pain. I swung my legs off the couch and set the pipe on the coffee table, next to the *Night Demons* book I'd rescued from the floor. An ache in my hand from gripping the pipe too tight in my sleep made me wince. I rubbed my hand and stood, gazing around my living room like it was an alien world painted in glaring butter.

I live in a townhouse condo called Captain's Landing. Most things in New Salem have some sort of sea name attached to them. Captain's Landing had a ship's wheel sign outside and a big iron anchor on the lawn, so it was impossible for tourists (locals didn't give a damn; they were used to New Salem's quirks) to miss the cheesy faux nautical design and hopefully be enticed into buying summer apartments.

I had Apartment #12. My living room was sunken, with one of those black-metal hooded gas fireplaces, a glass coffee table, sectional couch and an overstuffed chair that reminded me of the one that was my dad's favorite when he sat me on his lap to read to me. Ghost stories, can you believe it? Must be some sort of irony in that, but my favorite had always been *The Legend of Sleepy Hollow*, even at the tender age of six. I was a weird kid. I didn't find those type stories quite as fun now that I had run into some strange things with Arly—getting stretched on a rack and nearly sacrificed by Sorceresses will do that to you. Over in a corner was my spider plant, which I had named Bogey, and against the wall was an antique Singer sewing machine. Did I ever tell you I make my own costumes? Old style Burlesque stuff mostly. It's a hobby.

Anyway, three steps above the sunken living room was a dining area and small kitchen. To the right a carpeted stairway leading to the upstairs' rooms. The front door window was in the shape of a half-moon—I'd had the porthole style one replaced, because I couldn't stand it.

I absently gazed out through the slider. The patio was awash with blazing dawn. No sign of the monkey, thank God, because I wasn't in the mood. But of course most people thought it to be some sort of unwritten law little skull-faced monkeys only showed up in the dead of night, not in bright sunlight. Nothing scary happens in bright sunlight.

Well, those people never lived in New Salem. Evil crap could happen any old time of day.

For the moment I avoided looking at the object the monkey had left behind. I had set it on the coffee table and I got this boneheaded notion that not looking at it would somehow make it not real. I mean, I could have been dreaming the whole monkey thing, right? Monkeys weren't native to Maine. Especially skull-faced ones.

After standing there another two minutes I still couldn't convince myself of that. I knew it really had happened, that I hadn't been dreaming. A shiver made me bite into my lip. I sucked in a deep breath, then let it out slowly. Standing around denying the truth wasn't doing me any good. It wasn't doing Arly any good, either. I needed to find some sort of lead to him and dwelling on ghoulie monkeys leaving creepy presents, caller IDs flashing weird symbols and nursery rhyme phone calls wasn't going to get me any closer to finding him. At least not at this point.

I had to get my ass in motion and do something, anything that would give me a sense of taking action. The only problem was I had no idea where to start.

SEVEN

Reflections

7:15am...

Did I ever tell you that Arly and I are supposed to be getting married?

That's why all those boxes are sitting around my living room. Oh, it's not for a while yet—I was hoping for a Halloween wedding, if you can believe that. You'd think with all the creepy stuff that happens to us I'd be more traditional, but that's me, one big contradiction (I'd always loved Halloween as a kid, but that's before I found out monsters could be real). We have a storage facility on the premises, so I'd packed some of the things I wouldn't be needing for a while, like winter clothes and such so it'd be easier to move when the time comes. I know, maybe I'm jinxing myself by starting so early. I've never been known for my patience, but I'm excited.

As I stepped out onto the small beamed porch and locked my apartment door, I glanced down, noticing how the bright morning sunlight sparkled from the diamond on my finger, the engagement ring Arly had given me. I look at it a lot. I remember when I first discovered it on my finger, after...well, you can read all about that in GRIMM, so I won't bore you with it again.

Sometimes I still can't believe I'm getting married. I thought it would never happen. *Maybe it won't,* a worried voice inside me said, and my stomach dropped. What if something horrible had happened to him? What if the "gift" that witch said he has didn't protect him from what's out there this time?

And who even said it had to be something supernatural? There are plenty of nasty human threats and Arly is a retired cop, after all. He's made enemies.

I shivered and hugged myself. The May morning was a little cool, so after showering I'd dressed in my usual bulky blue sweater and jeans and only half-dried my hair before pulling it back into a ponytail. My small jean backpack I often carried instead of a purse draped over a shoulder, I went down the three steps and wandered down the slate-tiled walkway. I'd decided to go over to Arly's cottage again, because honestly I didn't know what else to do. There had to be something I was missing somewhere.

Oh, did I also mention Arly's a little older than me? Well, maybe a bit more than a little but he retired early from the New Salem Force because of his youngest son's murder, so it's not like he's a hundred or anything. Yeah, I know what some of you are thinking—I've heard it all before—daddy issues. But it's not like that. My relationship with my father was perfect before my parents died. It's just that I don't think age has any real meaning when you love someone. It's just a number and I don't care what others think or say. Being happy matters more and with Arly I am. And believe me, Arly can more than keep up, if you know what I mean. And that's despite the garbage he shovels into his mouth at the Lagoon and chases down with bourbon. I keep bugging him about eating better, but you know how that goes. For as impetuous as *I* am...Arly's ten times more stubborn.

Before I knew it I had reached my cherry-red Beretta. I fished my sunglasses out of my backpack because the sun was killing my eyes, then leaned against the car, for a moment thinking I might actually start crying. It was all so overwhelming sometimes. After everything that had happened with those witches...Jesus, you know I had this funny idea tragedies only happened once in a lifetime and once you were past them—even supernatural ones—that was it, smooth sailing. I was engaged, healthy enough for someone almost sacrificed to a demon and looking forward to things. How stupid is that? I knew better, but rose-colored glasses are a specialty of mine.

No, dammit, I had to get a grip! I'd been through more than one rough spot—and that's putting it mildly, believe me—in my life and I would get through this. We would get married if I had to turn over Hell to find him. I wasn't a little girl who fell apart because things got tough. I hadn't been that little girl since I cried out nearly every tear I had the day I lost my parents.

I gulped a deep breath of crisp air and opened the car door. I flung my backpack onto the passenger side, then climbed in after it. I had remembered to stuff the thing the monkey had given me into the front pouch. After I went to Arly's place, I figured that would be my next step, trying to find out what the hell that object meant.

EIGHT

Little Boxes on the Porchside

Oh, crap.

There was something sitting on Arly's front porch. The last time that happened it was a garbage bag full of body parts and the sight of anything there gave me the creeps. I took a deep breath and pulled my Beretta to a stop in Arly's driveway. The engine made some sounds I didn't care for—gobbly, chugging sounds and those are never good—as I turned it off. It had been doing that a lot lately and I'm pretty lame when it comes to keeping up with mechanical check-ups. I kept the car for sentimental reasons, but one of these days it was going to give up the ghost and strand me.

In New Salem it probably would be the only thing giving up a ghost anytime soon.

I noticed my legs were a little shakier than I would have admitted to anyone as I got out of the car. I flung the door shut after grabbing my backpack, assuring myself it was only because I hadn't had enough coffee, but not quite believing it.

Arly's place was a cottage-style house and we still weren't sure whether we were going to live here after we got married or look for a bigger place. I was thinking maybe Florida…

I shucked my sunglasses and stuffed them into my backpack, then forced myself to look toward the porch. I let out the breath I was holding.

It was only a small package, no bleeding Hefty bag, this time. I can't tell you how much better *that* made me feel. I'm really tired of stumbling over corpses.

I s'pose I'm just a lot more nervous than I'd normally be, what with Arly missing and only my future at stake. Heh, you'd think I'd be used to that kind of thing by now. Seems like since the Sisters everyday comes with something evil taking a bite out of my ass. But that's an exaggeration and I know it.

You think in some weird way I get off on this sort of thing? That maybe I'm one of those adrenaline junkies or something? Pete—he's the guy who owns the Red Lagoon, the topless place where I used to dance—always told me I needed therapy. Course, if he knew about some of the things Arly and I had seen…

Yeah, he'd still be right.

When I got up the steps, though, I got another one of those ugly feelings in the pit of my stomach. Because the damn package had my name on it.

Calm down, I told myself. *You're just jumping to conclusions.*

I was, wasn't I? I mean, Arly could have ordered something for me before he disappeared and had it sent to his house. That made more sense than…than, well, whatever it was I was about to piss myself over.

I grabbed the package—it was fairly small, only about six inches high and wide—then jammed a hand into my jeans pocket and pulled out the key Arly had given me to his place. After unlocking the door, I stuffed the key back in my pocket. Once inside I kicked the door shut, then set the package on the table. Arly's kitchen was quaint, which just means small in New Salem. I remember the first time I showed up here in the early morning. I had a bag of groceries and a big plan to get to Arly's heart through his stomach. I didn't know Arly wasn't a morning person. You should have seen the dumb look on his face when he opened the door. But don't tell him I said that. It was dumb-cute, you know? Not dumb-stupid.

I couldn't help the smile that tugged at my lips. Even during that horrible period there had been some happy times, hadn't there? As you might have guessed one breakfast didn't really do it, but our relationship got a hell of a lot stronger a bit after that. And by hell, I mean literally.

My attention went back to the box. I stared at it like an idiot for a minute. Early morning glare slashed through the windows in dusty arcs and fell across the package. Well, at least there was no blood dripping out of it.

After tossing my backpack onto the table, I went to the counter and pulled a knife from the rack on the wall, then went back to the package.

Maybe I shouldn't open it, I told myself. Maybe it was s'posed to be a surprise or something.

Why would your name be on the outside, then? another voice in me chimed in and never one for debate when I was curious I slashed the tape across the top.

I set the knife on the table and pried at the box flaps, getting them open.

You know those mouse-across-the-feet bleats I told you about before? Guess what came out of my mouth now?

NINE

Monkey Bones

Curious Skullface wasn't going to be scaring the hell out of me during any thunderstorms from now on.

Because in the box were bones.

Monkey bones.

No, I wasn't sure they came from the same monkey that had appeared on the patio and left an object on my apartment carpet, but I had a really funny feeling in the pit of my stomach they belonged to the creepy little bugger. And, yes, I did know for sure the bones belonged to a monkey. If I said I recognized the little skull face staring up at me you might think I was crazy, but that's exactly the case.

All right, you got me, probably all monkey skulls look alike but just take my word for it.

I stared at the bones, which looked somehow incredibly old. They weren't clean and white and they weren't bloody (boy, was I glad of that!) Just kind of a weathered brown. I had no desire to touch them and find out if they were brittle.

I slapped the box flaps shut and took a step backward from the table, staring at the damn box for maybe a minute, as if the bones might suddenly animate themselves and jump out. I'm brave like that sometimes, but honestly I'd had it up to here with monkeys for the moment, dead or alive.

I didn't get a long time to think about who might have sent them to me, or how they might have known where I would be to find them, which is probably a good thing given my suddenly frightened mood, because a sound came that made—you know, I hate to use the old cliché about blood running cold, but that probably describes it better than anything else I could think of at the moment.

It was a laugh. A little girl's laugh. It rose and fell with an echoy quality, not particularly frightening or malicious in itself, but still enough to make me think about peeing my pants again.

"Who are you?" I said and felt immediately stupid. Like it was going to answer, but somehow the sound of my own voice made me feel a tiny bit better.

As if in answer, the laugh came again, and this time it carried an innocent quality, like a child having fun at a game. It also carried a familiar quality and if it were possible for my blood to get any colder it did, then.

"Patricia?" I whispered, as if afraid it might actually answer me with a yes. "Patricia, is that you?" I looked about the kitchen, seeing no source from which the sound might have come. I had this foolish idea some neighborhood kid might have snuck into the house and hidden under the table, but I knew better.

The laugh stopped and a crushing silence filled the room. I stood alone again in the early morning light, a peculiar sadness replacing the sense of fear I had experienced a moment before. Ghost voice or no, I missed Patricia. I missed playing childhood games with her and I missed talking to her, confiding in her girlish things and connecting the way only twins could. A ball of emotion lodged in my throat. I swallowed at it but couldn't get it to leave.

It couldn't be her, I told myself. She would no longer be a child. And she wouldn't be in Arly's kitchen.

I was thinking that when the door suddenly rattled open behind me.

TEN

Dead Time for Bonzo

"**D**ammit, Johnny, you scared the hell out of me!" I blurted at the man who stood in the kitchen doorway.

"Sorry, Chlo, the door was unlocked, so I opened it quietly just in case." Detective John Sturdevant eased the door shut behind him and gave me one of those caught-with-your-finger-up your-nose smiles.

I nodded, forcing myself to calm a little. "In case of what?"

Detective John Sturdevant was one of Arly's closest friends from his cop days. He was younger than Arly, had a couple kids he constantly talked about, though they were in the custody of his ex-wife (he said it was better that way because with what his job entailed she could provide more stability. But when he talked about them it always came with the pain of being separated from their lives and all the things he was missing out on.) He'd gotten pretty deep into the Sisters of the Snake case, denying the existence of the supernatural practically the whole time—until he was forced to accept it. It had put a wedge of sorts between him and Arly, who had a hard enough time believing it himself, but they still would have died for one another. Sturdevant was a practical no-nonsense type cop who preferred muggers to witches, and I couldn't say I blamed him. At least he used to be. You can probably guess things have changed.

He stepped closer to the table, his gaze flicking to the box, then back to me. "Arlo gave me the key to his place after the...well, after what happened last December. I didn't know anyone else had one, except David, but I know they don't get on very well."

"David's a bit of a prick, to say the least." David was Arlo's oldest son, the living one, though some might have argued that point. He lives in Norwich, Maine, and has a problem with alcohol and attitude. I'd thought about calling him myself a few times, but the last time I talked to him about helping his father it hadn't been a very pleasant conversation.

Sturdevant smiled and fished a pack of Juicy Fruit out of his suit coat pocket. "So Arlo says. But he did end up helping with that whole Ficatier thing."

I sighed. "Arlo and I probably owe him our lives. Wish I could say that made me like him better…"

Sturdevant pulled a stick of gum from the pack and slid the rest back into his pocket. He unwrapped the piece, folded it over three times, then popped it into his mouth. The fruity scent of it filled my own nostrils and the memory of Patricia chewing that weird T-berry gum rose in my mind. That was one thing my twin sister and I had never had in common.

"I hear ya. I should have figured Arlo would give you a key, and I did see your car in the driveway, but after what happened last year I've learned not to take too much for granted."

"I could tell you a thing or two about that after that coma Ficatier put me in." I couldn't stop a shiver from shaking me visibly. Sturdevant gave me a sympathetic expression.

"Don't worry, last I knew that witch musket was back at the museum. It's harmless as long as none of the Sisters get hold of it and they're all gone, now."

Even though he tried to say it confidently I could hear the same note of doubt in his tone I felt in my gut.

"Are they gone, Johnny?"

I didn't like the flicker of fear that hit his face. "Course, they are, Chlo. You know what happened at the mansion. They have to be gone."

"And now Arly is." I choked back the ball of emotion swelling in my throat.

He shook his head, but some doubt still showed in his eyes. "This has to be something different. They failed in their mission. Even if somehow Ficatier got out, whoever she answers to wouldn't have tolerated such a monumental failure. Even Hell has its upper management."

I nodded, but I was still having a hard time convincing myself.

"Any word on Arly?" I asked without a shred of hope.

Sturdevant's confirming head shake still made my stomach plunge.

"Nothing. He might as well have stepped off the face of the earth. Nobody's seen him. I checked his usual haunts, The Red Lagoon, the Chinese place we always meet for lunch…no one has seen him in a week or more."

"I thought of calling David…"

"Me, too, and I probably will at some point, but you and I both know Arly wouldn't have gone to see him, not the way their relationship is."

He was right, but David did have certain abilities, ones he had likely inherited from his father, who he couldn't seem to be in the same room with for more than a minute before an argument broke out.

"You said the last time you talked to Arly he was looking for Patricia for me?" I folded my arms about myself, the memory of the phone call and that little girl's ghostly laugh invading my thoughts again.

Sturdevant nodded, snapped his gum. "Said he thought he might have found a lead, but didn't tell me what it was. He didn't want to get your hopes up until he knew more." He stared at me a moment and I could tell his intuition was picking up on my thoughts. Hell, I probably wasn't being too subtle. I'd never been good at hiding my emotions.

I shrugged, wondering if I should tell him what had happened with the phone call and ghost laugh. I knew he wouldn't like it.

He saved me the trouble, because his gaze went back to the box and I knew he'd noticed my name on the label.

"What's this?" Something in his tone said he didn't really want an answer, at least a weird answer.

"A box," I said stupidly.

He uttered a small laugh. "Not always hard to get things past me, but that much I figured out."

I smiled, but a sober mood quickly washed back over me. "I found it on the steps when I arrived. Somebody sent it here to me."

"You get packages here before?" He knew I hadn't but the cop in him made him ask.

I shook my head. "Never happened before. I was scared to open it."

He nodded, understanding a mirror of skulls in his eyes. "But you did, anyway."

"I did. Wish I hadn't."

"Something tells me I'm going to wish the same thing." He sighed. Deeply. "What's in it?"

"Monkey bones."

Now he just looked puzzled and a little relieved. "Monkey what?"

"Monkey bones. Not exactly QVC issue."

He cocked an eyebrow, then pulled back the box top flaps and frowned. "Looks like a monkey, all right, 'cept I don't like its face. Looks like—"

"I know what it looks like. A little monkey demon or something."

"Was gonna say, looks like the bones are really old."

"Oh." I think he wasn't going to say that but Sturdevant still had the need to deny the obvious sometimes. I guess I did, too.

"You know who sent it?"

I shook my head. "No idea."

"Who would know you might come here to find it?"

I shook my head again. "I get all my coffee club deliveries at home. Other than that nobody sends me much of anything."

"But someone has to know you have a connection to Arlo."

"I would guess."

"Any idea what it means? Kind of a peculiar thing to get in the mail unless you work in the Paleo department at a museum."

"No clue, but I've been having trouble with monkeys lately."

He gave me a look that said he wondered if all the supernatural crap I'd gone through last year hadn't made a few sandwiches fall out of my picnic basket.

"You wouldn't believe me and you probably wouldn't want to hear it," I said.

He seemed to deflate. "Aw, cripes, Chlo, not again."

"Again." I said with a nod. "I seem to have become a magnet for, you know…that kind of trouble."

He knew which kind I meant, of course. Weird crap, things that go bump in the night and sometimes even in the day and usually dragged anyone close to me in with it. He didn't look particularly pleased.

"I s'pose I should take this down to the lab." He peered at the box as if it had suddenly been sprayed by a skunk. He tugged a pair of blue surgical gloves from one of his pockets—which told me he had come here prepared in case he found some clue to Arly's disappearance he'd missed on his first visit.

"They look old but..."

He just looked at me and I made a face that wasn't all that far off from the one the monkey had made right before he dropped the—

"Oh, please, don't say it." His voice had that funny little hitch, the same one it got when the ghost of Granny Watson appeared on the TV set after the Sisters of the Snake murdered her.

ELEVEN

Friends Don't Let Friends Play with Monkeys

"**I** saw the monkey."

"What monkey?" He almost winced. He knew what was coming.

I ducked my chin at the box. "The one in that box."

He looked at me with that stupid expression again. "The one in *this* box?"

I think his voice went up an octave but I was uttering this nervous little chuckle myself to cover the fact that what I had just said sounded incredibly crazy and incredibly impossible.

I nodded. "That one in that box."

"But these are just bones, Chlo. And they look old, way too old to have been from something alive recently."

We both knew that statement was pretty ridiculous in light of what had happened a short time ago with the zombie that almost killed me.

"It's the same monkey, the one I saw in my apartment last night."

"*What?*" Now I was sure his voice had jumped an octave. "Last night?" Not only was fear and puzzlement on his face, but an unspoken "Are you crazy?" hung at the end of his words.

I bit my lower lip, looked at the floor, sighed, looked back up. "I couldn't sleep. I was down on the couch reading when the power went off during the storm. During a flash of lightning I saw something on my patio. That something started tapping on the glass."

"And that something was the monkey? The one in this box?" He didn't want to believe it, I could tell. But he did. Six months ago he might have passed it off as the ravings of a lunatic; he couldn't do that now, not in New Salem, not after the Sisters of the Snake."

"Only last night he had skin and fur and stuff."

"Well, that's a real big relief." His sarcasm was duly noted. "I mean, it would have been *much* worse if the bones were walking around on their own."

"Like worse hasn't happened in this town?" It just slipped out and he sobered immediately. I could tell he was just trying to keep his own sanity, which, if I guessed right, wasn't hanging on by a lot since tagging along with Arly and me.

"All monkeys look like." His tone didn't carry a lot of hope.

"I know it sounds crazy, but it's the same monkey. I'm sure of it."

"Monkeys aren't native to New Salem…" He kinda mumbled that. He was probably trying to talk himself into something, but it didn't help, if his gaze riveting back to the box were any indication.

"I'm aware of that. I have a sordid history with them."

"I hope that's some kind of joke aimed at your profession…"

I smiled, almost genuine. "It's not. None of my customers ever threw poop at me."

"So this monkey on your patio…" He looked back to me after flipping the box flaps shut.

"I call him Curious Skullface."

"Charming." He frowned. "Maybe he was just somebody's pet who got loose."

"People can't have monkeys as pets anymore."

"I'm aware of that, Chlo. I meant a trainer or something. Should be easy enough to check if there was a traveling circus in town who lost one."

"You won't find one who did because—"

"Because he's in this box."

I nodded. "Because he's in that box."

"And this monkey who was alive one minute then old bones the next, did he just run off or keep tapping on your window all night?"

"I let him in."

"You *what?*"

"I know, but I had a pipe. I figured I could brain him if something happened."

"He could have been rabid. Monkeys are fast and strong. You wouldn't have had a chance."

I sighed. I couldn't really think of anything to explain my stupidity. "I know. I kept telling myself I was like one of those stupid women in horror movies who know a psycho killer's lurking in the basement but they go down there just the same."

"That about covers it." He tried a grin. "No offense."

"You're lucky I'm too shaken up to take any. Anyway, he left me something."

Sturdevant twisted his face into this expression that said he really didn't want to hear anymore but knew he was going to listen anyway. "I should know better than to ask but what did he leave you?"

"This…" I grabbed my backpack from the table and unzipped a compartment.

TWELVE

Beware of Monkeys Bearing Gifts

After pulling the object out of my backpack I handed it to Sturdevant. He took it like I had just handed him something I'd pulled out of a medical waste bag, then relaxed after peering at it for a moment. His emotional sigh was almost audible.

"Looks old…" He turned it over in his hand.

"It is. Six-hundred years, I think. My parents told me they bought it at an antique shop in France."

He nodded, nothing dawning on him yet, but I knew it would. He was too good a detective for it not to. "Silver?"

"I think so. Or pewter, maybe. It's pretty tarnished." I glanced at the silver locket he held in his open palm, a heart trimmed with deep blue stones within raised *fleurs-de-lis.* "I think the stones are sapphires, but I'm only an expert where large diamonds are concerned." I winked at him as he glanced up at me, but he wasn't in the mood for humor and, really, neither was I. I could still hear that child's laugh in my head and see that monkey on my patio.

"This symbol…" He ran his index finger over the top of the locket. "It looks Chinese, maybe, or Middle Eastern."

I shrugged. "Mom and Dad never mentioned anything about what it could be when they bought it for my sister. I think they just thought it was pretty. They got me an antique doll. I used to collect them."

A memory came back to me and with it deep sadness welled in my heart. When Patricia and I were sent to the home we weren't allowed to bring much more than the clothes on our back. What happened to my doll collection, I never knew. I suddenly missed it, despite the dread in my stomach the reappearance of the locket in Sturdevant's hand dredged up.

Why did the locket's reappearance cause me dread? I think I was going to have to tell Sturdevant that now because a look flashed across his face. It wasn't a pleasant look; it was one that said, "Oh, crap, I just realized something bad."

"Wait a minute," he said, confirming the look. "Where'd you say you got this?"

I tried a smile but I'm pretty sure it came out constipated. "The monkey gave it to me."

His eyes narrowed ever so slightly. "The monkey you found on your patio...the one you let into your apartment and the one you now think is a bunch of Bonzo bones in that box?"

"Yeah, that one, Curious Skullface."

I could see the wheels turning behind his eyes. "But you just said your parents bought this for your sister in a shop in France."

"And you didn't even need to write it in your notebook to remember it." My sarcasm was wasted, but I'm not surprised. He had just renewed his membership in the there's-something-disturbing-going-on club.

"Oh, cripes." He started chewing his Juicy Fruit a hell of a lot faster, remaining silent for what seemed like an hour but was probably only a half a minute.

"It gets worse," I said when he didn't speak.

"I imagine it does." He paused, sighed, looked at the locket. "So you're telling me your parents bought this for your sister in France, what, how many years ago?"

"When we were six. My father took the whole family with him on a business trip."

"When you were six...and that was how long ago?" He was trying to be funny to alleviate his own dread, I think, but it fell flat.

"If I told you that you'd know my age." I winked again, but the tension remained thick. "I think how long doesn't really matter so much, anyway."

His face washed a bit paler. "No, what matters is the monkey gave it to you. How in the hell would he have gotten it?"

I saw him glance at the closed box on the table. I knew he was thinking about the bones and trying to reconcile them with the live monkey passing out antique lockets. I wish I had an answer that would have eased his mind, but I was fresh out of reality bites.

"The last time I saw it was when they took Patricia away from the home. She was wearing it."

"You're right, this is getting worse."

I ducked my chin at the locket. "Open it."

His look said he didn't want to, that he already had more than enough to ruin a good night's sleep, but he pried at the edges anyway, opening the locket.

Each interior side held a picture of a little girl.

"One of these your sister?"

I nodded. "The one on the left side is. The other is me. Hard to tell us apart looks-wise, but our personalities were a lot different."

"How so?"

A fragile smile drifted across my lips. "Pat was a lot more temperamental than I was. She was always kinda getting into things, being more rebellious."

He chuckled. "Says the woman who dances naked for a living."

"I came into my rebellion stage later on. Pat just seemed born with it."

He snapped the locket shut. "That still leaves the question of how it got from a child to a monkey some…how many years later?"

"Thirty," I said without thinking.

"And why he brought it to you…"

"Then ended up as bones in a box," I added.

He clearly didn't care for that last part. "That's not possible, Chlo."

"Was Angelique Ficatier?"

He groaned. I had him there. Three-hundred-year-old witches running around trying to raise demons weren't really the stuff of reality, either, yet it had happened.

He ignored the remark. "There's a woman at the New Salem Museum of Natural History—"

"Genie Lansing."

He frowned. "Yeah, that's her name. She gave Arlo the Inquisition sword to use against Ficatier. She might know what this symbol means." He ran his finger over the top of the locket again. "And she might know some of the history behind the piece. She seems versed on things French."

"And things supernatural."

"That, too. Worth asking her, anyway, though I don't know what it might have to do with Arlo's disappearance or how a monkey got your sister's jewelry."

"There's something else about that symbol…"

He let out another one of those long sighs that said he didn't like what was coming. "I've stopped being surprised…I think."

"That symbol on the locket appeared on my caller ID right before the monkey gave me the locket."

"I take it back, I'm still capable of being surprised, and not in a good way." He fiddled with the locket, not looking eager to hear the details.

"The power was out. My ID shouldn't have been working. But the symbol kept flashing across its screen."

"And the phone, was it ringing at the time?"

His tone told me he already knew I was going to say something he wasn't going to like. "I heard something on the other end, a little girl's voice singing a child's rhyme. The voice was distorted, like it was coming from a distance or filtered or something, but I swear it was my sister."

"But your sister wouldn't be a child now." That was the practical detective side of him in denial again.

"No, she'd be the same age as me."

"So it couldn't have been her."

"The ID box couldn't have been working and old monkey bones from a live Curious Skullface couldn't be in that box, either."

He didn't say anything for another minute, likely because there was nothing *to* say. When he finally spoke, his voice carried little conviction. "All the more reason to check with Lansing on that symbol."

"Arlo said she's a bit peculiar."

He nodded. "That she is. Call her first and set up an appointment. Be punctual; she's anal as hell." He handed me back the locket. I tucked it back into my backpack.

"I'll try her. Honestly, mostly because I have no idea what else to do."

His expression turned as serious as any I had ever seen on him. "I've been on the force a lot of years, Chlo, and frankly I have no idea where to look next, either." He grabbed the box of monkey bones from the table. "I'll take these to the lab for all the good it will do and keep trying to find out where Arlo last went, who he might have seen, but right now..."

I nodded, my heart heavy, then stared at the linoleum floor. "I know, Johnny..." My voice came out almost a whisper. "Believe me, I know." I looked up at him. "I'm trying to stay optimistic, trying to tell myself there's some reasonable explanation Arly left without saying anything to me, but..."

"But monkey bones and missing lockets showing up don't do a damn bit of good for your confidence..."

"No, they don't."

He nodded, an expression like a pallbearer's on his face, then turned and went to the door. He paused, after opening it, hand on the handle. "Thirty-six," he said.

"What?"

"Your age. Thirty-six." He smiled.

"Don't you have criminals to go beat with a hose or something?" I was a little irritated with myself because I realized he had taken advantage of my state of mind to trick me into giving out my age. I don't know why that even bothered me, other than maybe I subconsciously worried people would point out the difference in ages between myself and Arly even more if they knew an exact number.

"In New Salem?" he said, grinning. "We use stakes and wooden mallets for that." He chuckled and closed the door behind him.

I didn't stay annoyed with myself for long, because the moment after he left the child's laughter started again.

THIRTEEN

Haunting Me, Haunting You

The laughter seemed to be coming from everywhere in the house, not just the kitchen. A little girl's voice, echoy. It sent a shiver skittering down my back because I heard the voice even more distinctly this time and couldn't deny who it belonged to.

I remember a time just before my parents died when Patricia and I had wandered into the woods behind our home. Actually, not so much wandered, because Pat led me there. She was always doing stuff like that, mostly because my mother and father or some teacher told her not to. Like I told Sturdevant, Pat was the rebellious one (though if she knew what I did for a living she'd sure get a laugh out of it. Shy little Chloe, flashing her goodies for a bunch of drunk slobbering men. Maybe she would even be a little shocked and even as a kid that didn't happen to Pat very often. I almost let out a laugh myself, but at the moment I felt too haunted to appreciate the irony in it.)

Anyway, we spent about an hour in the woods going absolutely nowhere—Pat said she had a secret destination in mind and I would love it, but even at seven it didn't take me long to figure out she was full of crap and just wanted to go exploring because she'd been told not to leave the yard. And she wanted me along as her partner in crime for when we got caught, which we always did, since nine times out of ten I took the fall for it. My own fault, I s'pose; I should have known better, since she was always doing it to me.

You can probably see where this is going. We got lost. Pat was real good at getting us into trouble but when it came to getting us out…not so much. Well, maybe I should say she was good at getting herself out of trouble and leaving my ass in it.

An old guy who lived a few streets over happened to be in the woods at a stream, fishing. He found us and brought us back to my parents, whom he knew from a couple town hall meetings my father had attended. We tried to get him just to let us off at the top of our street, but he, being the Good Samaritan, insisted on bringing us to our doorstep. Of course, we couldn't tell Mr. Good Samaritan he had just assured us of being grounded for God knew how long and possibly a decent spanking.

I got the spanking. Pat somehow managed to screw her way out of it and make my dad believe it was all my big idea to go into the woods and that I had dragged her along. To this day I don't know how she got away with some of that crap. Not only wasn't I smart enough not to keep being led astray, but my folks weren't bright enough to figure out she was playing them. That's what I thought at the time, anyway. Now, I just have to wonder whether they weren't being harder on me because they thought I was the responsible one. I'm pretty sure they'd be spinning in their graves if they knew I took my clothes off for money.

Yes, I feel guilty about that sometimes, in case you're wondering, but that's something I'll talk about some other time. There are too many things I feel guilty about to get into them all now; it would take too long.

Anyway, the point of my story is after I got punished I told Pat, who got away with only a couple days grounding, and she'd laughed that same laugh I was hearing now. That fluttery annoying little chuckle she gave me when she knew I was pissed at her because she'd managed to lay all the blame at my doorstep again. I think there was a little bit of guilt mixed in it, but with Pat it was hard to tell.

Sometimes I wondered why I missed her tormenting me so much. It was so unfunny at the time I constantly wished I was an only child. Now, I miss every stupid joke she never played on me and every spanking I didn't get because she and my parents weren't in my life anymore.

The laugh came again, jerking me out of my thoughts, and I shivered.

"Pat?" I said in a much weaker voice than I intended. "Pat, is that you?"

The laugh grew stronger, crescendoing, then falling. I wrapped my arms about myself, telling myself again it could not be her, that she would no longer be a child. She would be my age, thirty-six, thank you very much, John Sturdevant.

The laugh had seemed louder and coming from the direction of the living room this time. I peered at the doorway leading to that room, thinking about that idiot horror movie girl with the psycho killer in the house again and wondering if I wasn't still that little girl who had followed her harebrained sister into the woods.

If you think I went toward the living room anyway…well, you're right. I did and I knew better, but trouble seems to have become—maybe it always was—my new profession.

Arly's living room looked kinda eerie or maybe it was just the ghostly voice weighing on my perception and mood. Sunlight sliced in dusty shafts through the partially opened blinds, falling in dagger patterns over the old cedar chest beneath the window and across the worn carpet. Otherwise the room was quaint, with a couch, large screen TV, end table, old brick fireplace against one wall and not a hell of a lot else. Arly wasn't big on clutter, unlike me, who liked the comfort of "stuff."

I stood there a moment, feeling…what? I guess the only way to describe it was the feeling you got as a kid when you had fallen half asleep in a darkened bedroom and you felt something from the closet slinking out and pulling on your blanket-covered toes. Whatever it was made your insides get all warm and squishy and made you want to pee the bed the moment you felt those blankets being tugged down along your body.

Then you'd wake up, of course, and everything would be ok because you'd realize it had only been one of those weird lucid dreams. I had that same feeling now, but the problem was I wasn't in one of those dreams and whatever was coming out of the closet was somehow weirdly real.

It sounds stupid. All right, I know that. But a lot of things sound that way since the Sisters of the Snake and stupid usually translates into someone getting hurt or killed because stupid isn't stupid, it's deadly. I know I am not making a lot of sense, but something just dawned on me and changed that slithery closet feeling to another sensation: dread. Because if that voice did belong to Pat, and if it really was a little girl's voice, that meant that Pat…

Was dead. She had died as a child and now I would never have my sister back.

No, it's not her, I told myself, because I felt tears coming.

"It's not you!" I yelled. I think I was yelling to convince myself and chase away the horrible feeling in my gut.

Chloe…(Chloe…Chloe…Chloe…)

"No…" I whispered, hearing Pat's voice come with another burst of laughter. This time there was a distant quality to it, like in the phone call I'd gotten during the storm.

Chloe…ring…ring-a-ring…of roses…

I froze, wanting desperately to be asleep, having a nightmare. I wasn't asleep. But I *was* in a nightmare.

"No, you can't be Pat! Who are you? Why are you doing this?"

A snap came from behind me and I let out a startled sound. I forced myself to turn, knowing I wasn't going to like what I was going to see…

FOURTEEN

Another Face, Another Rhyme

I suddenly wished I hadn't bought Arly that widescreen TV for Christmas.

An image flickered on the screen, faded, then with a snap came back again. The image was distorted, wavering, like in the old days when you tried to get in a distant station in using rabbit ears.

Ring-a-ring of roses...

Voices came from within the image, sounding as if they were echoing from a great distance, doubled, the sound of children singing an old nursery rhyme.

The little girl's laughter all about me stopped as the TV flashed on and I can't say that was really any comfort. Because last night when the monkey was tapping on my slider door I was scared, I mean, really scared. But now I was going beyond that to the verge of panic.

I've never been the type to run from something. I usually ran towards it, Arly would have told you, and he would have probably been right. If God passed out balls to females He had given me an extra set, I think (gotta have some big ones to flash your stuff in front of drunk drooling men, don't you?)

But right now any *cajones* I might have thought I had would have resembled those on the Polar Bear Club member first into the January New Salem ocean.

Yeah, I know, I'm lucky I didn't piss myself for real this time. I might have had I not been through so much with Arly and those Sisters of the Snake a few months back. But with as much as I went through—they'd damn near killed me, after all—it wasn't the same as this. With this I was frightened half out of my skin because it had a personal element to it. The laughter, the locket, the voices…

They all said: Pat, and that's who Arly had been trying to find for me before he disappeared.

I stood there like a frickin' potted plant, my stomach twisting around my backbone and my legs turning all rubbery and threatening to go in two different directions.

The image on the TV strengthened, retracted, grew stronger again.

Dammit, you're stronger than this, I told myself. *Pull it together.*

"No…" I shook my head as the image of a little girl formed on the screen. She stood in the center of other children who whirled in a circle, their hands linked, their faces utterly blank expanses of cellophane-like skin stretched over bleached bone. They somewhat resembled that stupid monkey, I thought, uttering a little chuckle against my will that made me think I might be losing it completely.

A pocket full of posies…

Their voices, so horribly sad now, so…*lost.*

I realized the distortion about them wasn't simply caused by a far-off signal trying to pull in. It was snow, swirling about them, pattering their thin flesh and the shreds of clothing that hung from their emaciated bodies.

No. Not snow. Ash. It was ash fluttering about them, ash drizzling from a gray void of a sky.

Beyond them loomed the grayish outlines of school equipment; monkey bars, slides, swing sets. They looked vaguely familiar, despite having no distinct outlines, something about their arrangement…

School. The schoolyard where Pat and I had played in first and second grade.

"Pat…" My voice came out a whisper, a shaky whisper, and I tried to force myself to move.

It can't be her…

The little girl standing in the center was the only one of the children with features…the same features Sturdevant would have recognized from the picture inside the locket.

Pat's features.

We…

Oh, please, God, this can't be happening…

All…

"Pat..." My voice came a bit louder, but still quivered. I didn't want to believe it was her, but that little girl standing in the middle of those whirling children looked so much like my sister it made my insides ache.

Fall...

She looked exactly the way I did at that age, exactly the way she had on that schoolyard when we would play that game.

Down...

The circle collapsed, the children falling to the ground, but it was no game, because somehow I knew those pathetic little skeletal figures without faces were never going to move again.

Ash drifted over them, forming a gray shroud from which wisps of charcoal smoke began to curl.

"Oh, Christ..." I said, shaking my head, fighting to keep my stomach from surging up into my throat.

Because a hissing sound came and their thin flesh began to bubble, great blisters forming.

I wanted to turn away. I really did. But I couldn't force myself to look from the horrible scene.

It took only a moment for the blisters on their flesh to erupt and when they did I saw no blood, simply dust, as if they had all been mummies crumbling under a scorching Egyptian sun.

Their flesh cracked in places, sloughed away, turning to dust as it hit the ground, then drifted off like smoke under a dark breeze.

A moment later they were nothing more than skeletons and those soon crumbled as well.

I felt like I was going to choke on my heart. It pounded in my throat and a horrendous sorrow I can't even put into words gripped my soul.

It wasn't real. It couldn't be real.

How many times had I thought those words over the past months since meeting Arly? Too damned many, I figured. And they still sounded just as stupid. But as much as Arly or I might have wanted to deny the things we had seen, we couldn't. The only other explanation was we had both gone insane together and right now I was so frickin' lucid I wished I *was* in a room in New Salem Memorial chewing on a crayon and mumbling Dr. Suess passages.

I wasn't insane. This wasn't a dream. But I still couldn't accept the little girl who now stood looking at me from the widescreen was my sister, Patricia.

Chloe...

I jerked from my thoughts as the little girl on the screen came forward. She was wearing an Easter dress, one I remembered my parents buying her—hers was yellow, with little lace flowers running along the collar and sleeves, and mine was blue. Her hands lifted and her palms flattened, as if she were pressing against the inside of the TV screen.

I'm not sure how I made it to the TV screen without falling on my face. It's just that one minute I was about to collapse and the next I was in front of the screen, kneeling, my hand pressed against hers.

"Pat..." I said, my voice so low I almost couldn't hear it. "Pat, it can't be you..."

Everything inside me was screaming at me it had to be some sort of trick. Ficatier had liked using tricks like this...

Ficatier's dead, I told myself, a sudden chill washing over me. I didn't feel reassured, because things didn't always stay dead in New Salem. You only need one zombie breaking into your apartment to figure that out.

Chloe...it's coming...

The voice was Pat's, at least the way I remembered Pat's voice being, though it was still somewhat distant, echoy.

"What, Pat? What's coming..."

Something began to form on her cheek. Blood. Tiny beads of blood rose, shaping into lines with transoms and sharp angles. The symbol that had appeared on my caller ID, the one on the locket.

The locket...you can't stop it...without...

Her voice faded and her face became semi-transparent as a great gust of ash swirled around her.

"No! Pat, don't go!" I yelled, tears welling in my eyes. "Arly, where's Arly?"

A sad expression crossed her face.

I...love you, Chloe...

A burst of laughter sounded from all around me and Pat's face on the screen suddenly changed. It came back to full strength and the expression was no longer that of a sad little child. The symbol on her cheek vanished. Pat's hands came away from the inside of the screen and she began to laugh in time with the voice echoing from all around the room. Her eyes turned into reflections of nothingness, jagged flashes of colorless anti-light exploding and dying within them. The eyes expanded and contracted, as if breathing. The little girl's expression pulled into a vicious smile.

You can't stop it...you can't stop us...

Pat's voice no longer held any hint of a little girl's tone, of innocence. It had become something awful, something evil.

"Who are you?" I said through clenched teeth. I don't think I have ever felt as angry as I did right at that moment, because though I told myself that couldn't have been my sister, part of me still clung to the lost little girl in that TV world as if it were, and this thing had just taken her away from me. Again.

"What have you done with her?" I shouted it this time and came to my feet, all feelings of fright suddenly gone, replaced by rage.

The image on the screen laughed and that laughter swelled within the room, mocking me.

You can't have her back...you can never have her back...

I lost it. I'm not ashamed to say it. I lost it completely and a moment later I had grabbed the lamp from the table beside the couch and hurled it at the screen.

A horrendous crash sounded and the image of the little girl and everything else within that TV world vanished with a jangling crash and not a little smoke. The laughter filling the room ceased at the same instant and the hush was almost as eerie.

I took deep breaths, struggling to calm myself. Two minutes later I had regained some of my composure and realized I had reacted on pure emotion. I should have questioned the girl behind the screen further, instead of losing my temper.

I also realized I was going to have to buy Arly a new TV.

"Chloe?" a voice came behind me and I whirled, looking for another lamp to hurl...

FIFTEEN

Evil is as Evil Does

"Jesus, Johnny, that's the second time this morning you've scared the crap out of me!" I set the second lamp I had grabbed back on the table and tried to swallow my heart.

Sturdevant just sorta stood there, looking about three shades paler than he had the first time I talked to him a few minutes ago. He didn't say anything. He just stared at the smoldering TV and I could tell from that I-just-crapped-a-bowling-ball look in his eyes he had seen something that wasn't going down well.

"Johnny?" I said, starting to get my nerves a bit more under control. I really should have been getting used to being startled by now, but I think it was only getting worse.

"Arlo's not gonna be happy about the TV," he mumbled at last, as if looking for something to say that made no mention of ghosts or witches or demons or skeleton monkeys that suddenly showed up on patios.

"I might have overreacted." I was pretty sure I hadn't but he had a point about the TV. That had cost me a couple weeks pay and replacing it while I wasn't dancing at the moment was a problem for another day.

He fumbled in a pocket and pulled out another stick of Juicy Fruit. His hands shook as he unwrapped the gum, then shoved the foil in his pocket and the stick into his mouth.

"I know better than to ask," he said after chewing the gum soft. "But you had a good reason for killing the big screen?"

I nodded, swallowing hard. "I had a good reason."

"It have anything to do with some kid laughing?"

"Uh-huh. You heard that?" I wrapped my arms about myself and shuddered a little shudder I hoped he didn't notice. He kept staring at the busted TV screen.

"I had just gotten to my car. I thought it was some kid outside and looked around but didn't find anything. Then I heard voices coming from inside the house. I figured you weren't talking to yourself."

"I'm not that far gone yet but if this stuff keeps happening..."

He nodded, some of the color coming back into his face. "Tell me about it. I came in to see you hurling a lamp at the TV. I only got a glimpse of what was on it."

"It was Patricia," I said before I could think about it or stop myself. "I told myself it wasn't her but..."

"Patricia would be your age, not some little girl, Chlo. And I got a notion she wouldn't be living inside Arlo's widescreen."

"That didn't stop Granny Watson from showing up on his old RCA."

His expression dropped a bit at that. He had seen the old woman's ghost appear during that Sisters of the Snake thing, and no matter how much he wanted to deny the supernatural what he'd seen with his own eyes was telling him otherwise.

"What did she want?"

"Patricia?" I said, still a bit addled. "I'm not sure exactly. She said something about someone or something coming, and mentioned the locket."

He seemed to deflate. "There's been enough of that sort of thing in New Salem the past nine or ten months. I'm sick of it."

I had no argument there. "It's like this town has gotten..." I shrugged, suppressing another one of those little shudders. "Infected or something."

"Makes me wonder about Ficatier and her brood. Maybe when they were trying to bring that demon back...maybe they let something else out."

"Or maybe things have always been this way since they started this town three-hundred years ago and we've just closed our eyes to it."

He laughed a nervous laugh. "Closed our eyes? I wish we could do that. I don't think we've closed our eyes to anything." He paused, looked at the floor and chewed his gum a bit too fast. When he looked back up a serious look stained his eyes that made me think of folks at a funeral viewing the corpse for the last time before it went into the ground. "Something's happening to this town, Chlo. I don't want to admit it to myself, and I don't think Arlo does, either, but New Salem's different. Maybe you're right, maybe it's always been this way. But before…something, I dunno what, maybe some veil or something, held them back…"

"Them?" I asked, knowing it was a stupid question.

"Whatever's trying to get through. I'm not sure Ficatier and her witches were the cause. I think they were a symptom. Or maybe an organism of the infection. If they had released Czcarabus…well, then it would have been over. But Arlo stopped them, at least temporarily."

"I don't like the word temporarily." My life had been filled with temporary, from my parents, to my sister, to lovers who had come and gone. That's something *I* was sick of.

His laugh was almost genuine this time. "I don't, either. But maybe they're being more subtle about it now. Maybe they're trying to break through in smaller ways, or maybe that veil has become too thin to hold all of them back."

"Again, I ask 'them'?"

"You know what I mean. Them, or him, or it, whatever it is that wants this town. The Evil."

"For a guy who didn't want to accept anything remotely dealing with the supernatural, you sure came down with a bad case of horror-movie syndrome."

He walked to the window, with two fingers pried apart the blinds and peered out. "I don't know how to put it into words. This is all…new to me. I'd like it to stop."

I frowned. "It's not going to."

He gave me a little nod and looked back at me with that bowling-ball-crapping look. "I'm afraid of that, Chlo. I'm not ashamed to admit it. I'm just a small-town detective. I'm not equipped to handle things like this, either emotionally or in my job. And if we don't find Arlo I'll be even more afraid."

That I could relate to. Arly had something special about him, but he was missing. And instead of making progress finding him I was being hounded by something I didn't understand. I had no idea whether it related to his disappearance or if maybe my own longing for my missing sister hadn't somehow brought it…well, whatever it was on the TV, to me.

"You have no idea what…" he hesitated and I could see he didn't want to say her name, but had little way around it. "Pat was trying to say about the locket?"

"No."

"You're not telling me everything…" He frowned and his forehead turned into a network of worried little crinkles.

That's why he was the detective and I wasn't, I thought. He had read between lines when I didn't even realize there were lines.

"I didn't want to believe it was Pat. But I started to…Christ, I don't know, maybe I always did deep down. But there was something else about her…"

He let out the heaviest sigh I think I have heard out of anyone. "Something else?"

I nodded, walked away from the TV set and leaned against the fireplace mantle. I peered at the tri-frame holding the pictures of Arly and his two sons, David and Bobby. Jesus, I missed him. I just wanted to fall into his arms and hide from the world and from whatever darkness had come into our lives. But I couldn't and that made me even more sad.

"It's like it was Pat, then it wasn't. Something else took over. Or maybe she was trying to reach me and something stopped her."

"But if that's true, then Pat…" He let the words die.

"I know what it means." Pat was dead and I had no chance of ever finding my sister again, unless it was under a gravestone. "But whatever it was that took over it was…like you said, evil. It told me I would never have her back and I could not stop what was coming."

"What was coming…" It wasn't really a question.

"It wasn't specific."

"Evil things never are."

"Ain't that the truth. They like the game as much as the goal, I think. They like taunting. Evil's a cocky bastard."

His laugh was a bit more relaxed and I could tell he was getting used to the idea weird things were happening again. Me, I had no choice but to get used to them.

"I don't know what to do next, John." I felt tears wanting to flood my eyes. Dammit, I wished I could just cry. It would be so much easier not to have to hold up all the time. I wished I was as tough as I made myself out to be.

"Maybe there's nowhere *to* go. It's not like we have forensic evidence or witnesses, clues to follow."

"Not the type you're used to on the force, anyway," I said.

"That's the trouble with evil. Too much waiting around for the big ugly to happen." He was trying to be funny but the seriousness in his tone just made it sound awkward.

"I think I need a coffee. Or anything to take my mind off of this for a few minutes or an hour." I was starting to shake.

He nodded. "Follow me over to the diner on Maple. After, you can go see Lansing and I can go drop off the monkey bones."

The way he said it made it sound almost routine.

Too bad routine hadn't been on the docket in New Salem for far too long now.

SIXTEEN

I Dream of Genie

The coffee hadn't done anything to sooth my jangled nerves. I don't think it did much for Sturdevant's composure, either. Like he said, he was just a small town detective and things that went bump in the day weren't his jurisdiction. They weren't mine, either. At least they hadn't been until Angelique Ficatier and her damn Sisters of the Snake.

And now this. Now Arly was missing and my twin sister Pat was appearing on TV sets, a Pat who was still a child. A Pat who might have brought something else far more dark with her, or perhaps was part of the Big Dark. I didn't really know what to think. I was having enough trouble denying it *was* Pat when everything inside me now screamed the opposite.

And I had nothing much to go on to point me in a direction to Arly or my sister. I had a monkey showing up out of nowhere—a monkey who might have been a freakin' monkey-boo, for that matter, and was now old bones in a box—a weird whatever taking over my sister on a TV screen and giving me the standard horror movie crap warning…and a locket that used to belong to Pat. How had the monkey gotten it? Why had he given it to me? What did it mean? Was Pat dead and now a ghost? Was the coffee at the diner too damn expensive for the swill it tasted like?

You can tell I was getting myself a little wound up here, right? I mean, I'm entitled to be a little on edge—Christ, a lot on edge—after everything that has happened, aren't I? I'm entitled to have questions whirling through my mind making me tighter than one of my old G-strings, am I not? I think I am, especially with God-knows-what might have happened to Arly.

I got a brief flash of all my wedding plans going down the drain and felt a little guilty. What's important was finding him, not dwelling on the stupid fairy tale wedding I had planned since I was kid.

"Dammit!" I yelled suddenly, with the heel of my hand smacking the Beretta's steering wheel.

Ouch. That hurt. And brought me back to reality in time to avoid getting side-swiped as I drove along the waterfront. A lemon-head (I can say that, I'm blonde) in her daddy's graduation present laid on her horn and gave me a one-fingered peace sign. I was tempted to give it right back to her, but it had been my fault, so I just looked straight ahead and pretended I hadn't seen it.

Funny, that slamming the steering wheel thing always worked for Arly but I think my hand was starting to swell and I felt suddenly pretty stupid. I was just so worried and frustrated and I had little hope that seeing this Genie Lansing person at the museum was going to do much good. Yeah, she had helped Arly with that sword and Miss I-Wanna-Marry-a-Demon Ficatier a few months back, but I didn't really see how she could help me find him now. Maybe she could tell me something about the locket, but I didn't even know if the two were connected and wasn't sure I cared. I just wanted the supernatural to leave me alone. I just wanted to be married and living happily ever after. Or at least the way most people lived. Without witches. Without ghosts and demons. Without Evil.

I was tempted to smack the steering wheel again but my throbbing hand made me think better of it.

I glanced left before I signaled to turn onto a small side street that would take me up toward the museum, noticing the Red Lagoon hadn't opened yet. Pete usually opened later in the afternoon. Strippers liked to sleep late. I knew I was going to have to pay him a visit after I got done with Lansing and the thought of it made me a little more nervous than it should have. I had changed a lot in the past six months or more. I didn't really understand it but falling in love with Arly, nearly being killed on more than one occasion…it makes you think about your life and your priorities.

The New Salem Museum of Natural History was entirely too modern a building for the old style brick and brownstone, Colonial and Victorian types of houses prevalent in the old neighborhoods of town.

The thing was an architect's nightmare of abstract archways and peculiar angles. Stringy neon lights in pink and green boasted its name on a salmon-colored stucco wall. The place was crammed between two smaller office buildings at least fifty years old, which made its ugliness stick out even more.

I pulled up as soon as I found a free meter, whipped off my sunglasses and stuck them in my jean backpack. I grabbed the backpack as I got out of the car. After slamming the door, I dropped a quarter into the meter and headed for the museum entrance.

The interior was as vomit-inducing as the exterior, with recently redone tiled flooring you couldn't look at for too long without wanting to grab a bucket. Who the hell does a floor in tie-dye anyway? The pink and green neon light strings on the walls only made it worse.

I made a face and walked to the reception desk before I could think about how many of my tax dollars had gone into this collision of ancient exhibits and acid-trip design.

A young woman with short spiked hair looked up from behind the desk as I approached.

"Yeah?" she said in a tone that kinda pissed me off.

"I'm Chloe Everson. I called about meeting with your director, Genie Lansing."

The girl gave me a look that probably would have made Rosie O'Donnell orgasm but only annoyed me further.

"It's 10:15..." She glanced at a Minnie Mouse watch on her wrist. I didn't like her attitude. It reminded me of those snobby little tweaks with their $15,000 front porches who somehow figured being an exotic dancer was loftier than being a stripper, semantics aside. The type that came to Pete looking for temporary jobs, despite the fact they thought they were better than the rest of us dancers, because they needed the extra cash to pay for necessities while their regular paychecks went up their noses.

I checked my watch, gave her the nasty little smile I reserved for those girls. "It certainly is. And you didn't even need a digital to figure it out."

Her look changed. It wasn't a good change. It was a change that said I was close to getting my second middle finger in the space of ten minutes.

"You're late by fifteen minutes," she said, as if I had just missed the deadline on a nuclear treaty pact. "Ms. Lansing doesn't do late."

I think my blood pressure jumped fifty points. "Well, I don't do rude, sweetie. Consider yourself lucky I've got too many other things on my mind to waste time rearranging your attitude."

She ignored my tone. "You'll have to come back some other time. Call and make an appointment and don't be late."

She probably thought she dismissed me with that, but by now my temper had replaced my worry and fear. I thumped my backpack on the desktop, sighed and put on the look I gave those bitch kitties who thought their crap didn't stink.

"It's a small bag," I said, ducking my chin at my backpack. "But I'm pretty sure if you piss me off any more than you have already you'll need a proctologist to remove from where I cram it."

Yeah, yeah, yeah, I know it sounds stupid but with the tone I used the tweak hesitated and I could tell she was wondering whether the cougar standing before her was serious, and insane enough to actually do it. She flinched. Just a nick. But enough for me to know I had intimidated her. I'd been in the stripping business a long time and just because I had a soft outer shell didn't mean I wasn't rock candy inside when I needed to be.

I don't know what the girl would have answered because the intercom on her desk squawked.

"Let her through," a woman's voice came from the speaker and the look on the young woman's face wasn't what I would have called pleased. I did see a trace of relief, though. The cougar still had it, I congratulated myself.

"Yes, Ms. Lansing," the young woman said, her voice a lot more sugary with the woman on the other end. She looked up at me. "Go down the hall all the way to the end. She's in her office. Knock first."

Then she looked at her desk and began fiddling with papers.

I thought about a sarcastic "thank you" but didn't bother. Instead, I grabbed my backpack and headed around the desk to a long hallway. From the corner of my eye I noticed the tweak watching my ass. Well, what the hell, I had paid a lot for these jeans.

The hall was almost like walking through an alien world. Rooms lined either side, labeled for various time period displays. I noted the witches room Arly had told me about, and a small shudder went through me because it brought back some unpleasant memories of Ficatier.

When I reached the office I knocked and a voice answered from within, telling me to enter.

I opened the door to see a young woman standing in front of a desk.

SEVENTEEN

Genie in a Locket

I didn't like the bitch the moment I saw her.

Something about her, I dunno what it was, but I took an instant dislike and if the prissy little smile on her lips was any indication the feeling was mutual. If I hadn't known better I would have tagged it as jealousy—I'd seen it on enough strippers, for chrissakes—but I figured that was too out-of-context to be accurate.

She stood in front of a small desk cluttered with papers and some artifacts I didn't recognize. They certainly looked old but that was as far as my knowledge of that sort of thing went. The woman herself was petite, maybe about ten years younger than me, dressed in a loose flower-print skirt that hung just low enough beneath her knees to satisfy a nun's taste and a shapeless blue top that might have been chic for a lady pirate. Multi-colored plastic bracelets on her wrists gave her a peculiar Sixties flavor that clashed with her jaunty Catholic ensemble—yes, I'm being sarcastic and petty, but like I said, I automatically disliked her. An elastic band encircled her right ankle. I had no clue what *that* fashion statement was s'posed to say.

Her hair was this weird white-blonde, more a lack of color than anything else, cut in a pixie style, strands curling in about her cheeks and beneath her small chin. Her eyes were weird, almost colorless, with a misty marbled look. Oh, and they said something: "I'm pissed off."

"You're late," Lansing said, the pissed off look in her eyes leaking into her voice.

"Yeah, I got that from your receptionist," I answered in much the same tone, letting her know I was in no particular mood to be screwed with.

The prissy little smile dropped off her thin lips and her eyes narrowed. "Your call said something about a locket?"

Ah, ok, all business, this one. She wasn't about to engage in a bitch kitty match, at least not at this point. That's good, because pissing off a stripper is never a good idea, no matter how smart the other woman thinks she is.

I shrugged my backpack up higher onto my shoulder. "That and any information you might have about Arlo, Miss Lansing."

"Ms." she said, and the irritation in her tone increased. I was now certain she liked me as much as I liked her and the catty little jealous twist was back on her lips.

That made me wonder. It had come with Arly's name, hadn't it? But she was young enough to be his daughter, maybe even granddaughter. I took enough crap for having daddy issues, but here was little Miss—excuse me, *Ms* I Dream of Pixie crushin' on my man. I would have burst out laughing but something about her made it not the least bit funny.

"*Ms.*" I said, putting a little sarcasm into it.

An intensity came into her eyes, and I wasn't sure why. "Arlo Grimm?"

Well, duh, I wanted to say, but instead settled for, "The one and only. He's been missing for over a week now."

Her eyes got a weird intense look. I didn't care much for that, but I might be biased because I didn't much care for anything about the woman.

"I haven't seen Arlo since before Christmas."

Oh, so now we were on a first name basis? No Mr. Grimm, just Arlo? I suddenly got that same jealous twist to my lips I'd seen on hers. I'm not sure why.

Another emotion came with it: disappointment. I had hoped somehow I would walk in here and she would say she had seen Arly recently, had some information pointing to where he might have gone. It would have saved me from some of the darker thoughts brewing in my subconscious.

"You haven't heard from him at all?" My voice reflected my disappointment but her attitude didn't soften.

"You said something about a locket?" she repeated, and the lack of concern made my blood heat.

"Arly's missing, *Ms.* Lansing. I haven't seen him in over a week and now…weird stuff has been happening again. I'm sure he told you all about Ficatier and her little demon-raising party."

"I did give him the sword, after all, Miss Everson."

I had a powerful urge to let out an "Arrrgggh!" at her patronizing tone, but refrained. You got more with sugar than vinegar, as the saying went.

"The police can't find him, either," I continued, not sure why it was suddenly important to me to impress upon Pixie Sticks the seriousness of Arly's disappearance.

"Maybe he got tired of you," she said and now I was really p-o'd. And that stupid jealous tilt was back on her lips. I had half an urge to slap it off her.

I sighed, getting myself under a bit better control. I was letting this woman get to me and I think mostly it was because I was already worried and scared. Usually I handled her type better.

"I was hoping you could tell me something that might indicate where he might have gone, but if you can't I won't bother wasting anymore of your time."

Another kind of smile this time. I wasn't sure what it was but I didn't like it. Spite and victory mixed, maybe. She thought she had won something, though what that something was escaped me.

"Please, Miss Everson, let me see the locket. I have a busy schedule."

I debated just walking out and telling her to go to hell, but, crap, I was already here and if that locket and those weird occurrences had anything to do with Arly's disappearance I couldn't afford to pass up any opportunities.

I went to her desk, brushed aside some of the junk, which brought a satisfying startled look to Lansing's face. I unzipped a compartment after plunking the jean backpack on the desk and fished out the locket.

She took it from me, glanced at it. "The locket of Rouen."

"The what now?" I asked. Sorry, history wasn't my forte.

Her expression became somewhat complacent, her misty marble eyes momentarily distant. Then she looked back to me, face serious, all trace of cattiness and challenge gone. "Fifteenth century, French."

"I know it's French." I said it with a that kind of insecure inflection that came when somebody who knew more about a subject wanted to throw it in your face and you had to pretend you weren't a complete moron. "It belonged to my sister. My parents got it for her from an antique shop in France when we were kids."

She opened the locket; her misty marble eyes focused on the pictures inside, then she snapped it shut."

"My sister and I," I told her, though she hadn't showed any curiosity as to whom the pictures belonged.

She nodded as if she already knew. "What, then, do you want from me?" She passed me back the locket.

That was the problem: I wasn't sure *what* I wanted. I guess I had hoped she could tell me if it related to Arly somehow and just what was happening to me.

"A monkey gave it to me," I blurted before I could stop myself.

"A monkey gave it to you," she repeated as if she were talking to a patient at a mental hospital.

"A little one, capuchin, I think. He was on my patio during the storm last night. I let him in and he dropped the locket on the carpet."

"Lucky that's all he dropped on the carpet," she said. I think it was some attempt at a joke but her delivery sucked and she wasn't exactly Ellen. "There are no monkeys native to New Salem."

All right, I was just getting more and more irritated. The urge to slap her came back. "I'm aware of that, but the monkey's dead now so I guess it doesn't matter."

She almost grinned. "The monkey's dead..."

Why was I feeling like an idiot child hauled up in front of the teacher's desk? "Someone sent me his bones in a box and now Detective Sturdevant has them."

You know, I probably shouldn't have told her that, because saying it aloud only made it sound sillier than it already did in my head.

She nodded. "Someone..." she muttered. I didn't like that hint of concern that came into her tone, because it said, not someone, some- *thing*.

I debated telling her about Pat's appearance on the TV and the warning I'd been given but I had a feeling it wouldn't have helped the Are-you-crazy? look she was already giving me.

"All right, forget about the monkey." I took back the locket, tucked it into the backpack and zipped the flap. "What about that symbol on the locket, what does that mean?"

Her face didn't change. It told me she knew exactly what that symbol was and I had finally hit on at least something that might prove useful.

"It's Arcadaeic." She moved around the desk, then lowered herself into the thick-cushioned office chair. Her bracelets clacked as she leaned her elbows on the desktop.

"Look, it's obvious I have no idea what that means, so why don't you jut drop the attitude and explain things in layman's terms."

She peered at me intently. "You're a stripper, right?"

I nodded, wondering why the hell she had asked. "I'm not embarrassed by that."

"I suppose you are not."

Ok, another jump up the piss meter.

"You disapprove?"

She gave a causal flick of her hand. "You would think women would have come farther in the past six-hundred years than being toys for men."

Ok, I could hear the righteous, holier-than-thou inflection clearly and *that* was something I was use to dealing with. And you know what? I didn't give a damn. I've explained my reasons for doing what I do and what someone else thought about it, especially uptight little Ms. Pixie Sticks, didn't bother me in the least. At least it was everyday stuff. Nothing supernatural about having a stick up your ass.

"The symbol?" I prodded and maybe it annoyed her that I hadn't gone for her bait.

"Arcadaeic."

"You said that already. "I don't know what that means."

"No, I suppose you wouldn't." She sighed and it was forceful enough to rustle the papers on her desk. "It's an unknown language, said to have been used between the warriors of Christ and Lucifer as they met in battle. The symbol is one of protection, given to a few...*humans,* who, for lack of a better term, the Forces of Good deemed...different, special in some way. People like your Arlo Grimm. It's much like the Hindu symbol the Nazis adapted for their Swastika."

Well, I had to give her credit. She suddenly sounded like a professor in an old monster movie but she did say "your" Arlo, meaning mine. I don't know why that pleased me. On the other hand, what she was telling me didn't add anything toward finding him, and maybe even made me a little more nervous about what that apparition on the TV set had told me.

"Let me get this right, you're saying a locket with a symbol from an unknown language spoken by Good and Evil is just floating around the civilized world instead of sitting in some collector's display case or buried under the Vatican or somewhere like that?"

She flashed me a put-out frown, like I should have known the answer. "It is an unknown language and as such is mistaken for an artistic expression. That is why it was in an antique shop."

And a monkey would have it, why? I wanted to ask, but didn't. The monkey angle wasn't gaining me any points. I suddenly had no desire to mention I had seen the same symbol on my caller ID, either. "So if it's an unknown language how do you know what it says?"

She said nothing for a moment, and I got the impression she was struggling to find an explanation that would make sense. I also sensed the crazy shoe was suddenly on somebody else's foot.

"I've made it my life's work to know such things, Miss Everson."

Ok, that just sounded stupid. How old was this woman, anyway, in her twenties or eighty? Because she sounded suddenly way older than she looked.

I grabbed the backpack from the desk, exasperation riding my nerves. I got the distinct impression our meeting was over and I could see now why Arly and Sturdevant had warned me that this woman was odd. She was more than odd, but I guess if your hobby is sitting in a stuffy office sifting through ancient artifacts all day your social skills probably suffered along the way.

I went to the door, wishing I had gotten more than I did, but at least now I knew what the symbol meant, though that didn't really explain why a monkey had given it to me or why something that might have been my sister seemed to want me to keep it.

"Miss Everson," I heard behind me as I grasped the door handle.

I turned back to her and she had a peculiar distant look on her face.

"That locket...it was...*rumored* to have been made for Joan of Arc."

And that was s'posed to mean what to me?

"How do you know that?"

"It's my job to know that."

Great, Avoidance 101 again. "You said that symbol was one of pro-tection? Didn't do her a hell of a lot of good, did it?"

The look that crossed her face was unreadable but I knew it wasn't something good. It was something dark, but beyond that I had no clue.

"It was stolen from her before she was burned."

I bet it wasn't part of her job to know *that*, I almost said, but what good would it have done?

I nodded, stepped from the room, leaving the door open about six inches as I did so.

EIGHTEEN

Monkey Jinx

I paused in the hallway about halfway down and let out the shudder that had crawled up inside me. I am not sure why I felt the need to do that, but I did. Despite the fact I now knew what the symbol on the locket meant—and on my caller ID, which still freaked me out—what did I really have? And how did it get me closer to finding out what had happened to Arly?

The answer was—it pretty much got me closer to nothing. On second thought, I think that's why the shudder came. Because I knew I was still a thousand miles from nowhere. So the locket might have belonged to Joan of Arc. Big deal. Joan of Arc died, what, six-hundred years ago? What could she possibly have to do with Arly? Or the apparition that appeared on the widescreen?

I couldn't see a connection. Not that in this town that meant there was none, but like I told you yesterday I'm not the detective. I'm the stripper and right now I felt naked in ways I had no control over.

I couldn't fall apart, I told myself. I couldn't lose it now or I'd be worse off than I was already.

Did Lansing know more than she was telling me? The thought suddenly sprang into my head. I took a shuddery breath. How could she? She was the one who had given me some cockamamie story about protection symbols and dead martyrs. The woman admitted she hadn't seen Arly in months. And it was clear neither of us cared for one another, so maybe the curator had just been screwing with me. And then there was that whole little jealousy thing.

I sloughed my backpack off my shoulder and unzipped the compartment holding the locket. I fished out the locket and stared at it a moment, not sure exactly why I was even bothering. I jammed a nail in the crack between the sides and opened it, gazed at the pictures of myself and my sister as children.

"What does this all mean, Pat?" I whispered, still not entirely sure I believed what I had heard and seen was really her. "What does this locket have to do with Arly?"

Nothing, my rational mind told me and my stomach sank a bit further. Like the nothing I had gotten from Lansing and the nothing that was going to give me a nervous breakdown if I let it.

I snapped the locket shut and stuffed it into the backpack, then zipped the compartment shut. Whatever the case, I was going to have to decide what to do next because if I sat around dwelling on what little chance I had of finding Arly I was going to go crazy.

*Maybe you already have…*a voice came back to me from somewhere in the depths of my mind. Maybe everything I'd heard and seen, or thought I'd heard and seen, was just me losing it. Maybe everything Ficatier and her Sisters of the Snake had put me through had turned my mind to Silly Putty.

Sturdevant saw it too…

Oh, yeah.

He couldn't have been going crazy with me at the exact same moment, could he?

I let out a small laugh that held absolutely no humor. This was New Salem, I reminded myself. Anything could happen.

I forced myself to take a step forward. The whole creepy atmosphere of the museum wasn't helping matters.

I made it only a handful of steps before I stopped.

I had heard a noise. Not a laugh this time but an entirely familiar little chitter of a thing.

"Oh, you've gotta be kidding me…" I mumbled and eased around, afraid to see what I knew would be there.

I was right and I couldn't help the wobble that went through my legs.

It sat in front of Genie Lansing's partially opened office door. Looking at me. Its forehead doing that creepy crinkly thing.

The monkey.

NINETEEN

What monkey?

"**O**k, that's not possible," I said. "You're in a box." Pretty stupid, since the furry little reject was sitting there mocking me in his crinkly forehead way.

I stood still an instant, debating whether to turn and run, or go kick his fuzzy little ass. I decided the latter sounded more satisfying.

"Ok, you…" I muttered and started for him. Probably didn't take monkey ESP to figure out I was sick of his crap, because he whirled and skittered into Genie Lansing's office. I half-expected to hear a shriek come from the room, but nothing.

I reached the door and shoved it inward.

And stood staring for what seemed like an hour but was probably only a few minutes.

Not only wasn't the monkey anywhere in sight, but I saw no sign of Genie Lansing. Monkeys are small. He could have been hiding under the desk, hanging from a light, whatever. But Genie Lansing didn't have that option. She was gone and there were no other exits from the room. Only the front door. And she could not have come out that way. I would have heard her.

"What the hell?" I mumbled, then searched the office thoroughly in case the monkey was hiding somewhere. He wasn't. Both were gone. Somehow.

You know that feeling you sometimes get when you step on a grave? I got that one now. It started in my heels and shuddered right on up to the crown of my head. My first reaction was to look for reasonable explanations. I spotted a wall vent, about ten by six inches. The monkey could have crawled into that?

Yeah, and used a little screwdriver to undo the screws, then somehow squeeze his hand back through the little slats to screw them back in again. That made sense.

And Lansing was waaay too big to go out that way.

That left me with explanations I didn't really want to think about.

It also left me with another thought. What if that monkey belonged to Lansing? What if she had sent him to give me the locket, knowing I would eventually wind up here asking her about it? For what reason?

There's something she wasn't telling you...

That was the only thing I could think of.

But then why send the monkey bones to Arly's addressed to me? If Lansing owned the monkey, then...

Those bones were a warning from some*thing* else. Something opposing Lansing? Maybe. I had seen a peculiar look on her face when I mentioned them. Now that look made sense.

I thunked my backpack on the desk and fished out my cell phone. My fingers shook a little as I located the personal cell number Sturdevant had given me. It took three rings for him to answer.

I could tell by the way he answered his mood wasn't particularly good.

"I'm at Lansing's, Johnny." I said. "Something weird happened."

I heard a nervous chuckle. "Not that that surprises me, but I have something weird for you, too."

"Let me guess, it has something to do with those monkey bones."

"How'd you know?"

I frowned. "A capuchin told me. You know how old the bones are yet?"

"No, I gave them to Strigger in forensics. They have to be sent to a lab for dating, but he thought in the 500-600-year range just looking at them. Problem is when he went to send them they had disappeared."

"What do you mean 'disappeared'?"

"The box, the bones. Gone. He said he set them on a counter to pack them up and went off for a coffee. When he got back they were gone. No one in the station took them and they didn't just get up and walk away."

"The monkey was here, Johnny. I saw him. He ran into Lansing's office and disappeared. She did, too."

"She what?"

"Poof."

"That's not possible."

"You're tellin' me?" I hung up with Sturdevant and gave the office one last scan. The deeper I got into whatever was going on here the less I liked it.

I had the feeling things were only going to get worse.

TWENTY

Old Haunts

As I drove along the waterfront I couldn't get rid of the feeling Genie Lansing had been hiding something and that the monkey belonged to her. Had she sent Curious Skullface to give me the locket? I would have bet on it, but why hadn't she simply explained her reasoning earlier instead of the cryptic crap? That was the trouble with supernatural stuff; it all came in riddles. Nobody, Good or Bad used a direct line.

One thing I did know: the more I thought about that woman, the less I liked her. And she didn't have much on deposit in that bank to begin with.

And now the monkey bones were missing, not that they could have told me much anyway. Those, I am certain, were a counter to Lansing, a warning. Again with the cryptic stuff. And again I got the thought Evil just enjoyed the Game far too much.

My gaze focused back on the road ahead as my front tire thumped over one of the old trolley tracks that were still embedded in the blacktop along the waterfront. I saw the sign for Gibson's Antiques, which wasn't more than a few blocks from the Red Lagoon and butterflies suddenly fluttered in my stomach.

I think I told you I had stopped stripping recently, right? But I never told you why. I guess it was because the closer I got to Arly and with our engagement I had started to feel like I didn't need it anymore. I mean, it was good money, more than I could make sitting behind a desk in an office but I had started to change inside and the sense of control I needed over men had begun to fade. With what I had with

Arly, I felt...well, I felt like I wanted to surrender that control. Because with him it felt...*mutual*, is the only word I could put to it.

I had planned to be sending out résumés over the past week and taking something that paid enough to cover my rent up until we got married and moved in together. So I had told Pete—he owns the Red Lagoon—I was taking a leave of absence. But then Arly had gone missing. And I found myself not only without much of a desire to spend my time job hunting but needing the flexibility in hours stripping gave me to search for Arly. The supernatural didn't have much respect for scheduling.

I had some money stashed away—actually a good chunk—but it wouldn't last forever, either. So I found myself without a lot of options. Stripping gave me freedom to come and go as I needed—Pete was good about that and a friend of Arly's, so he'd understand if I needed to take off at a moment's notice—plus it would pay my bills, at least until I found Arly.

Or didn't.

The thought made me shudder.

Did I miss it, you might ask? Stripping, I mean. I guess maybe I did in some ways. You don't do something like that for as long as I have and not feel some separation anxiety. But that type of career wears on you too. Hell, some girls it eats up completely because they get into drugs and alcohol and...well, *other* things. I was never like that, but since you now know my age it's obvious I can't do it forever. No matter how good a shape I'm in, things start droppin' sooner or later.

Pete was going to be surprised to see me so soon, I think.

The waterfront was littered with shoppes, canneries, a marina, old factories, bars and the usual tourist-trap souvenir places. Traffic was kinda light, but New Salem is not a large town, only around 50,000 people, I think.

I blinked. Something horridly chilled went through my insides.

Because now...

Now all the traffic had vanished. There was just...nothing. No cars, no people. The sides of buildings suddenly looked blurry, distorted in a way I can't explain, buzzing with some formless fluttering anti-light.

The trolley tracks and blacktop had also disappeared. Now I saw only an endless expanse of gray cobblestones and the car shuddered over each of them.

And snow.

Drifting out of a formless colorless sky.

I stamped on the brakes and rolled down the window, looked up. No, not snow. Gray flakes. Flakes that lazed down onto the cobble-stones and skittered along as if they had a life of their own.

I got out of the car, everything inside me wanting to come apart. I knelt, touched the flakes. Ash. Not snow; ash.

Ashes, ashes…

Children's voices, rising in the swirling ash. Singing that nursery rhyme.

Death…everyone…all fall down…

Laughter echoed from all around me, a child's.

"Patricia?" I yelled, suddenly more scared than I wanted to admit. "Why are you doing this?"

I probably should have asked "how", because if I hadn't known better I might have thought I was tripping, but I had seen too many weird things since Ficatier not to question the hows, only the whys.

I saw her, then. Standing about a hundred feet down the road. Patricia, the ash dancing about her, sizzling over her Easter dress, which was gray now, hanging on her small frame.

But it wasn't really Patricia, was it? No, it was the thing that had appeared over her on the TV screen, superimposed on an innocent face. Its eyes glowed with anti-light and it walked toward me, a decep-tively fragile thing.

Its hand lifted, finger pointing at me and I got the sudden urge to jump back in my car and lock the doors. Like that would have helped.

No, I would stand my ground. I wasn't going to let any pint-sized whatever get the better of me.

"What do you want?" I yelled at it. "Stop playing games!"

I forced myself to take a step towards the demon girl, and it stopped, as if surprised I had stood up to it. At least that's what I wanted to think. It might have just been getting ready to toast me.

You can't stop us…

No mouth movement came from the little girl but I knew the words came from her. The anti-light in her eyes blazed stronger. She started forward again and I panicked. I reached into the car and grabbed my backpack. My fingers shook like hell as I whisked open the pouch and grabbed the locket. Protection, Lansing had said. I had no faith in that but there wasn't a hell of a lot else I could think of doing.

Everything vanished.

The little demon girl, the laughter, the ashes falling from the colorless sky.

And everything came back, including a bunch of blaring horns and swearing drivers because I was standing in the middle of the street.

"Oh, crap," I muttered and heat rushed into my face. I jumped back into the car, not even attempting to try to apologize. What would I say, a demon girl made me do it?

TWENTY-ONE

The Old Bump and Grind

The Red Lagoon hadn't changed much since I'd last been in it, but I did see Pete had added a pole to the stage that jutted out into the center of the room. Above the stage the huge twin speakers were silent, but on it a young woman with small perky breasts practiced her routine on the pole. I didn't recognize her, so she must have been a recent hire.

The Red Lagoon was New Salem's only topless joint, pretty tame as far as these places go. It's where I met Arly. At this time of the day it wasn't open for business but I saw Pete behind the bar, setting up glasses. He smiled when he saw me approaching.

"Chlo! What's shakin'?" he said. He was a large man with too much belly weight but a good guy and every stripper's dad. He watched out for us. Nobody touched his girls, and Arly backed that up.

I gave him a half-hearted smile, though hiding the nerves I fought from my encounter in the street a few minutes ago wasn't easy. I was still shaken and I bet my face was three shades of pale.

"Like the song, says, Pete, the hips don't lie."

"Good to hear, Chloe. Wasn't sure I'd see you back here again." Ah, a note of hope in his voice. That was good.

I got right to the point. "Need a favor, Pete."

"Name it, Chlo."

"Need my old job back, at least temporarily?"

"The corporate world not treating you right?" he asked with a twinkle in his tone.

I thumped my backpack on the bartop, then slid onto a stool. "No, haven't even gotten time to pursue anything. I need the flexibility of the club back, for a short time, anyway."

"What's going on, Chloe? I know that look. Saw it back—"

"I know, back with Ficatier and her winged monkeys." I frowned. "Might be on the same level."

Pete's face dropped. He didn't know a lot about what had happened, but he knew enough to be worried. "Christ, not again. What's going on in this town?"

"That's the million-dollar question, isn't it?"

He cocked an eyebrow. "Arlo...I haven't seen him in more than a week. I got a whole freezer of grease burgers goin' to snow."

I felt like crying. Again. But I didn't. "He's missing, Pete. That's why I need the flexibility of this job, so I can hunt for him."

"Have you called the police?"

It was a natural question but I gave him a look of "duh" anyway. "They can't find any leads."

"Do you have any?"

I shrugged. "Not sure, just a bunch of weird stuff that may or may not be connected."

"Weird stuff follows you around now."

"Sure seems to, doesn't it?"

"Like flies on crap."

"That's very delicate, Pete."

He grinned. "My wife says I got a way with words."

"You're a smoothie, I'll give you that." I flashed him a warm smile. "Thanks for letting me come back."

"Door's always open to you, Chlo, you know that."

I nodded, slid off the stool. "See you tonight, then." I started walking away.

"Chlo?" I heard him say behind me.

I turned my head back to him. "Yeah?"

"You find Arlo. Find him safe. He's like a brother to me."

"That's the plan, Pete. That's the plan."

I was home about fifteen minutes later, not only feeling the jitters over what had happened with the demon girl in the street on the waterfront and missing the hell out of Arly, but also stricken with a weird sense of depression at having to go back to stripping. I never thought I would feel that way. I guess it was because I had thought I was leaving an old life behind, getting ready to start a new one by marrying Arly. But now everything just seemed...the same.

I know I am being a bit of an ingrate and should be counting my blessings Pete had given me my job back just like that. But I couldn't help it. And where before I kind of enjoyed the power whipping my top off gave me over men, now I felt a little…embarrassed. Weird. I'd get over it once I got back into the routine but even so it was a feeling I never thought I would have again.

It took me another fifteen minutes to get changed into some lose clothing and a sweat band.

On the second floor of my townhouse apartment I had a bedroom I had converted into a small dance studio. I'd put in a ballet bar on one wall and a rollaway dance floor, plus I had a kick-ass sound system in the corner. Afternoon light lanced through the windows, shafts filled with twirling dust, reminding me I hadn't bothered cleaning up in here because I had planned to use it as storage for a little while instead of a studio.

An annoyed grumble greeted me as I switched on the CD player, the annoyed grumble only a cat roused out a nap can make. I gave Puddin' Head a "don't-go-there" look because my mood was already south of the border. Puddin' Head belonged to Granny Watson until the Sisters of the Snake murdered her. I had adopted him. He was a huge tabby that looked more like a steroid-enhanced Tribble and sometimes his personality was a lot like Martha Stewart's, but I had gotten attached to him. He never hesitated to give me his opinion, though, and right now his opinion told me he'd planned a nap day and wasn't appreciating the noise of me starting a dance routine again.

He groaned one of those cat groans, then heaved his furry bulk off the pillow I'd put in the corner for him and padded from the room.

"Critics…" I mumbled.

I placed a CD into the machine and frowned again, not looking forward to how sore I was going to feel tomorrow or how many drunks were going to be ogling my boobs tonight, but put into perspective those things were probably the least of my worries for the moment.

TWENTY-TWO

Old Flames, New Haunts

1:00am...

I closed the door to my townhouse apartment and pressed my back against it. Just standing there in the dark, I took deep breaths and fought against the exhaustion and dark emotions crawling through my system.

Going back to work had been harder than I thought. It was bad enough the guys seemed a little drunker than usual tonight and Pete had threatened to take a baseball bat to two of them, but the thought of the Red Lagoon and my job having been where I first met Arly had played on my nerves all night. A ball of emotion lodged in my throat and tears swelled in my eyes. Jesus, I missed him. I guess I hadn't realized quite how dependant I'd become on his being there when I wanted to call, when I needed someone to talk to. All those little things you take for granted when you're in a relationship...

All those could be taken in a single instant and leave you wondering how you had ever gotten along without them.

Stop it! I told myself, sniffling. *Just stop it! You'll find him. You know you will. Just don't lose it. That's what they want.*

They?

Just who the hell were they, anyway? The demon girl had said "us", hadn't she? Did she mean a collective Evil or did she have demon pals?

I forced the thought from my mind and snapped on the light switch on the wall next to me. The chandelier above the table in the raised

---

dining room to my right came on, stinging my eyes. I pressed my lids shut, shoving myself away from the front door at the same time.

I opened my eyes slowly, locked the front door, then tossed my backpack and keys onto the table. With a heavy sigh I grabbed a diet Coke from the fridge and descended the three steps to the living room. I flicked on the table lamp and stared at all the boxes, deeper feelings of sadness washing over me. More plans and dreams mocking me. And nowhere to turn, no assurance that Arly was even…alive.

I felt like crying again, but I forced myself not to. I didn't even know my next step and everything seemed to be crushing me but I had to keep myself together. It wouldn't help to fall apart now.

I knew I would have to keep telling myself that because I was certain things would get a whole lot worse before they got better. They always did in New Salem.

An annoyed groan came from the corner and I saw Puddin' Head giving me the hairy kitty eyeball from his throw pillow. He had one in every room, did I tell you that? He'd made it pretty clear he owned the place *and* me, not the other way around. I let him think that. I'd get even when it came bath day.

"I'm not in the mood," I said to him, going over and giving him a pat. I had a feeling he either could tell my stern tone wasn't serious or he just didn't give a damn, probably the latter. Cats.

I heard a slight tapping on the slider doors and suppressed a shiver. If it was another damn ghost monkey…but no, it was just a few dime-sized raindrops hitting the glass. No thunder this time, anyway, and I was thankful for that, because if the power went off now I just might let out a shriek.

I went to the sectional and dropped onto it, every muscle feeling leaden, acutely aware of my perfumed sweat. I should take a shower, but the thought that bad things happened to chesty blondes in showers in horror movies didn't motivate me any. I'd put up with myself until morning. No one got murdered in the shower in the morning, did they?

After setting my Coke on the coffee table next to my copy of *Night Demons* I located the remote in the cushions and flicked on the TV. The late news was on, probably as depressing as always but at least it was some noise. My ears were still a little dull from the blaring music at the Lagoon anyway. An Asian woman reporter had just finished interviewing some doctor or something from New Salem Memorial:

...the latest outbreak of the mysterious disease that has hospitalized four people in New Salem over the past week. Doctors caution everyone not to panic until they locate its cause. The disease is characterized by eruptions of sores across the face and body that leak pus, nausea and vomiting, and a curious darkening of the skin. So far the victims have all been homeless men from the waterfront area.

In other news, a second waterfront murder appears to be the work of the New Salem Ripper...

I flicked it off. Noise or no noise, disease and murder were too much. I didn't need anything that gloomy right now.

I heaved myself off the couch and a heavier pounding of rain brought my attention back to the slider doors.

That's when I saw Arly and let out a scream...

TWENTY-THREE

Little Miss Demonic

I caught myself screaming and forced it to stop. It was just an automatic reaction but I was freaking myself out worse than I already was.

I shuddered. Hard. Grabbed myself with both arms and squeezed to stop myself from falling apart.

"Arly..." I whispered, waves of emotion at seeing him now overwhelming me and forcing back some of the fear.

I stared at the slider door, because Arly wasn't just standing on the patio beyond it, he was embedded in the glass itself, his image barely discernable within the rain streaming down the pane. He was semi-transparent and he was kneeling, naked, his wrists manacled to something above and behind him I couldn't see.

Did I ever tell you what Arly looked like? Although he's older than me you'd hardly know it. He runs and works out a lot to wear off all those greasy burgers Pete feeds him and the pizza he buys by the truckload. I think that crappy bourbon he puts down preserves him too, but he has a young face, a kind face—when he's not pissed off—kind of like Lee Majors from that old show where he was part machine. An older version, but not too much older.

But his face now showed more strain and hopelessness than I had ever seen on it, even with all the stuff that went on with Ficatier and her witches. His cheeks were hollow and his eyes dark, incredibly sad. It wasn't natural on him. But it was brief. His image faded a second, then came back, weaker, as if it were having trouble remaining. One of his hands reached out, fingers splayed, stopped by the shackle, though I heard no sound of iron clanking.

Chloe...help...me...Saint...Patricia...

I wasn't certain whether I had really heard his voice or if it had been just in my mind, because some of the words had been missing and rain suddenly roared down, turning the glass to a wavering streaking sheet of reflected light from my living room and darkness from outside.

Then the little girl's ghostly laugh started again, just as I took a step closer to the window. It rose and fell in a demonic wave, a mocking quality to it, a taunt.

He doesn't belong to you anymore...he belongs to us...we will use his gift...

That voice I heard distinctly and it was the damn demon girl again. A flash of a thought went through my head. The locket was in my backpack on the dining room table and I wondered if I could get to it. I also wondered if it would really do any good if I could.

The demonic girl's image coalesced within the glass, her eyes sparkling with anti-light, her face incredibly pale, almost a sickly green, a reflection of every vile emotion I could think of.

"What the hell do you want?" I screamed at her. "Tell me where he is!"

More laughter came from the girl and her lips spread in a spiteful grin. I saw something in her hands then, which were cupped near her waist. She turned her hands over, dumping bones from them, monkey bones.

She can't help you, either...She was too late six-hundred years ago...you will be too late now...ashes, ashes...

Who the hell was the demon talking about? I wondered. Lansing? Lansing wasn't six-hundred years old. Granted she was a bit haggard for her age...

"Where is he?" I asked, trying not to piss myself and stand up to the thing.

Another laugh came from the demon girl.

He tried to reach you...he had help, but that won't happen again...

What did she mean by help? Had Patricia found Arly? Had she tried to help him get a message to me?

The thought was stopped dead because the phone rang and scared the living crap right out of me.

I spun, stared at it on the end table. I saw the caller ID flashing and froze. There was no number showing up on the read-out; it was that frickin' symbol again, the one on the locket.

Forcing myself to move, I ran for the phone and snatched it up.

"Patricia?" I damn near yelled into the mouthpiece.

Ring-a-ring of roses...all fall down...

Children's voices again, singing the nursery rhyme. My mind started to whirl and I knew I would lose it if I didn't focus.

"What do you want?" I shouted at the phone and the line suddenly went dead. I slammed the phone down and whirled back to face the slider but the glass appeared normal now. Rain streaked down the pane but no demon girl and no Arly were within the glass.

TWENTY-FOUR

Reflections in a Locket

4:00am…

It took me more than an hour to get my nerves back under control after the appearance of Arly and the demon girl in the slider glass. I was probably still a hair away from going through the ceiling if anything else startled me, but at least I didn't feel so much like puking or crying at the moment.

I sat at the vanity in my bedroom, the small light to the left turned low, my chin resting in my hands and my elbows jammed into the vanity top. I wore my blue terrycloth robe and had pulled my hair back into a ponytail. I just stared at my haggard reflection in the mirror. I wasn't tired, despite the dark half-circles nesting beneath my eyes and the drawn look to my cheeks. To be honest, I was a little afraid to go to sleep. And my mind was still locked on the horrific image of Arly in the glass. He had looked so…helpless, I guess would be the word, and if you knew Arly you knew that was way out of character. He was the strong one, the guy who had chased down the witches, the guy I had started to depend on, maybe way more than I should have. You know? Because depending on people wasn't something that had ever worked out well for me in my life. Depending on people usually just translated to losing them. In the worst possible way.

Had I lost him now, too?

No, I couldn't let myself think that. He had tried to reach me and the demon girl told me he had gotten help from somewhere.

Patricia?

That was my guess. But it hadn't been enough and now all I had was a few words he had whispered before vanishing, and those words meant nothing tangible to me. They didn't tell me where he was, at least not as far as I could see. But maybe they told me the one thing I really needed to focus on: they told me he was still alive. Lansing had told Arly there was something "special" about him, something that enabled him to prevail against the Sisters of the Snake and made him valuable to them when they wanted to resurrect Czcarabus. Maybe that's why he was still alive now; maybe whatever that little girl demon was, she needed him for something.

But she didn't need me, did she? Why hadn't she just killed me?

Because I had the locket?

My gaze traveled downward to the locket, which lay on the vanity top before me. I had taken it out of my backpack before coming upstairs to my room, just in case that demon girl wanted it or some monkey broke in and decided to take it back.

I realize how dumb that sounds, but like I said, in New Salem…well, don't take anything for granted.

I picked up the locket and pried it open. As I gazed at the two pictures, myself and Pat, a deep loneliness and sense of loss washed through me.

"Are you dead, Pat?" I whispered, something in my belly clutching. "Are you trying to reach me and help Arly?"

And did it mean I would never find her again, never know the sister I had lost so many years ago?

Goddammit!

I snapped the locket shut and forced the tears gathering in my eyes not to flow. Even so, one trickled down my left cheek. A ball of emotion lodged in my throat.

It wasn't bad enough Arly had vanished. It wasn't bad enough some demonic rugrat had shown up and started tormenting me. But now something was telling me I would never get to see my sister alive again, either.

Life was a bitch sometimes. And it was a worse bitch the moment you let yourself even think about being a little bit happy.

I noticed myself clenching my teeth and my jaw muscles starting to ache and forced myself to take a deep breath. I was letting the negative get the better of me because I was lonely and scared and at my wits' end. I had to focus on the positive, that Arly was alive and trying to reach out, that Pat was trying to help and that if the damn demon girl had wanted me dead I would have been in an urn by now. Maybe it wasn't entirely the locket; maybe I had something special, too.

Arly always told me I did. And in New Salem that wasn't necessarily a good thing because with it came a bunch of things that went bump in the night. And Arly and I were a magnet for them.

Well, demons or monkeys, no one was getting this locket. It might be the only thing I had of Pat's, other than my childhood memories. If they wanted the locket they were going to have to take it off my cold...

Oh, crap, maybe it was better not to think about it that way.

I slipped the locket around my neck and peered at my reflection in the vanity mirror. The locket looked natural there, somehow, and it almost felt warm against the cold chill crawling around inside my soul.

Tomorrow was a new day and maybe if I made myself sleep I would have a clearer head and be able to figure out some sort of direction. I knew one thing, M-S Lansing wasn't going to find herself getting off the hook quite so easy, because my dislike for her and suspicions she was holding something back had gotten to a near paranoid level after a day of demon girls and dead monkeys running amuck.

I stood, sighing, turned to the bed. Puddin' Head was snoring on the left-hand side. He had staked his claim there nearly an hour ago and hadn't moved. He was taking up way more space than a cat should have needed and was unabashedly blasé about it. I wondered sometimes why I had gotten so attached to that cat. As far as cats went, he had arrogance and entitlement down to an art form. I just shook my head. He didn't bother acknowledging me but a paw flicked and I wondered if I had just been flipped the cat finger.

I shucked my terrycloth robe and draped it over the chair. I had on an old over-sized T-shirt with a Supergirl symbol across the front—yeah, I know it wasn't going to help, but anything to feel the least bit empowered, ya know? I usually sleep naked—no complaints from Arly on that when he stays over!—but tonight I felt vulnerable. Things, and I do mean *things*, were coming and going pretty freely in my apartment, so why give them a free show? Girls who did that in the horror movies usually ended up as stalker meat, so I saw no need to push my luck.

I switched off the light, knowing more than just literally I was in the dark and things might not get the least bit brighter with the morning light.

TWENTY-FIVE

Demons, Monkeys and Rats, Oh My!

Can somebody please tell me why I always end up naked on these cases?

I mean, really, I'm used to being naked. Probably nine times out of ten I feel more comfortable out of clothes than in them. But you know what happens to naked girls in horror movies? They are right there in line with Miss-I'm-too-stupid-to-stay-out-of-the-cellar, Miss Naughty Bitch and the Gimp to be offed first by the killer in the hockey mask.

And why is it you have to be naked *and* freezing before some butthead with an axe or a butcher knife appears?

Ok, so I maybe wasn't *totally* naked. I did have on my stripper's thong. *Pffft!* Like that was going to keep Evil from drooling over my naughty bits.

Somehow, I was on the street that runs through the waterfront in New Salem. I had no idea how I got there, why I was there, or how the hell to get the hell out of there. Indistinct light came from somewhere yet nowhere; I saw no street lamps. A serpentine mist slithered along the street and the ground felt lumpy and freezing beneath my bare feet. Cobblestones, I think. Like I was on the street back a hundred years ago. That didn't make me feel any better and I let out a shiver that would have sobered even the worst drunk at the Red Lagoon, considering my present lack of clothing. Speaking of the Lagoon, I didn't see it anywhere. Or any of the other buildings normally lining the waterfront, for that matter. All the buildings to either side of me looked dark, old and leaning, almost arcing inward at their tops. Windows were black glass, reflecting nothing. Some were boarded shut and there were signs nailed to some buildings. At first I couldn't make out what was written on them because they shimmered, blurry, but finally I got it: Quarantine, the signs said.

Another shiver and I wrapped my arms about myself, making sure I covered as much of my boobs as possible. Normally I am not the least bit shy about hauling out the girls but I had a feeling something was watching me that wasn't....human. Something dirty. Something that wanted to see every part of me with its black slithering tongue.

Ok, maybe I am being a bit dramatic but if you had been naked running around in the snow a few months ago with a witch chasing you, you'd be dramatic too. Really, you would. Trust me.

Sounds. Something...at first I thought it was laughter, and it was, at least partly. I heard the demon girl laughing again, somewhat distant, hollow, echoing through the dark canyon of the street. But another sound mixed with it...far off screams. Screams of utter agony and hopelessness.

Another shiver, even stronger than the first.

My first urge was to join in the screaming since my nerves had just about reached breaking point, but I choked it back. My second urge was to shout out, "Where the hell am I?" but I got the idea neither option would do me any good whatsoever.

I started moving forward, clutching myself even tighter, gooseflesh crawling on my body and my breathing getting shallow. The chilled cobblestones chewed at my feet. My heart banged against my ribs like some frantic troll pounding to get out of me.

I became suddenly aware of something moving within the mist but couldn't see what it was. But it gave me a rising wave of dread in the pit of my stomach.

An odor drifted to my nostrils, sickly sweet, like singed meat. At almost the same instant ash started drifting from the sky and I looked up. The sky was utterly black, endless. The flakes, gray and hissing, swirled from its depths. They didn't burn as they touched my skin, but the sound alone was enough to make me start.

To my right was an alley. I was certain it hadn't been there a moment ago, before I looked up at the black sky, because light flickered from it, orange and sickly yellow. I moved towards it, immediately backing off the moment I looked within. The light came from flames, their ribbony light cavorting with shadow on the building walls like lovers embraced in orgasmic frenzy.

I had all I could do to keep the nausea flooding my stomach from surging into my throat. I jammed a hand over my mouth and nose, forgoing modesty, because keeping myself from puking and covering my nostrils against the sickly sweet burning odor was suddenly the priority.

Now I knew what caused that ghastly stench: bodies. Burning bodies. They were heaped one upon the other, at least twenty of them, flesh charred and bubbling, hands reaching out, blackened mouths uttering horrible moans and shrieks. Flame, unsympathetic to their awful pleas, devoured their hair and skin. Boiling blood burst from their eyes, ears and nostrils. Black smoke billowed into the ebony sky.

Help us…please…help us…

I mumbled something against my hand, not sure what, as I backed farther away into the street, knowing I was a heartbeat away from hurling or maybe just losing my mind completely. I could no longer look at them; everything inside me wanted to scream and run and force the horrible sight from my mind.

Ring-a-ring of roses…

Children's voices suddenly emanated from everywhere, yet nowhere. I could not see them but had the sense they waited behind the walls of the dark buildings, watching, praying, crying; singing, hoping, dying.

Again things were moving within the mist and as I looked down the scream I'd been suppressing surged up from the depths of my soul and cut loose against the hand I still had clamped about my mouth and nose.

As I stumbled a few steps backward to get away from the things skittering in the mist I pulled my hand from my mouth and wrapped my arms about my breasts again.

I saw what moved within the mist now: Rats. Hundreds of them. Squeaking, darting, scaring the living hell right out of me. I hated rats, especially these huge wharf rats that populated the waterfront. They were like evil naked squirrels. That's what my mother had called them when I was a kid and as far as I was concerned it was accurate.

One of them leaped and I reacted. I would have made a punter proud because my bare foot sent that little bastard flying a good thirty feet, ass-first. The very touch of it against my skin made me shudder, but a small measure of satisfaction came with the sight of the thing rebounding from a building wall.

But there were too many of them and they made the mist seem a gray living carpet, converging on me.

Ahead two things appeared and the scream I had made against my hand now launched full throttle. I swear it stopped the rats for an instant.

"Arly!" I yelled, forgetting my fear and starting towards him, despite the rodents.

Chloe...help...me...Saint...Patricia...

He had appeared in the street, his naked body semi-solid, bruised and battered, face drawn, with welts criss-crossing his forehead and cheeks. Blood dribbled from the corner of his mouth. He tried to reach for me but something stopped him, shackles that vanished into nowhere above and behind him. Before I could reach him, he vanished. Just like that. And I think my heart and hope stopped for just a moment.

"Nooooo!" I yelled. But he was gone. Again. And in his place was the little demon girl, somehow obscene in a tattered Easter dress. Her face appeared greenish even in the indistinct light. Rings bubbled on her features, grew black and pieces of her flesh flaked off, whirling away into the ash drizzling from the sky.

"Ashes, ashes," she said, her voice heavy and hollow, only vaguely like that of a little girl.

"Give him back to me!" I yelled it before I could think and it was stupid but what else do you say in that type of a situation? You don't ask a demon for its green card and "would you like your meat grilled or broiled?" is out of the question.

Oh, did I tell you I'm prone to babbling and saying dumb things when I get really rattled? Now you know.

Around me the rats swarmed closer. They circled, leaping out of the mist, jaws snapping, barely missing me with their rotted yellow teeth. I kicked at them, missed one, launched another. Too many.

"Give up, Miss Everson," the demon said, the voice even deeper this time. "You can't beat us. And you can't have him back. We need him for what's coming. You didn't think *He* would entrust everything to Ficatier, did you?"

"What the hell are you?" I screamed at her/it. It came from fright but the only thing that scared me worse than rats was snakes, so ugly demon girls and supernatural boos took a distant third.

"You didn't really think he could stop us all, did you?" the demon girl said, drifting forward.

In the alley behind me a wailing ululated through the night. The demon girl laughed and it sounded like goblins sawing a fiddle.

The stench of burning flesh grew stronger. My legs threatened to go in two different directions and my head started to dance.

The rats grew more agitated, closing the circle. I felt their wire-bristle fur scratching my legs.

I was going to pass out. I know I was. I felt it coming on in a cold black wave. And once I did those rats would...

It suddenly dawned on me I had put on the locket before going to bed. My hand went to my throat. I felt cool metal and clutched it like I was grabbing a log in a raging river.

Then sat bolt upright in bed, a scream still on my lips.

TWENTY-SIX

M-S Demon

6am...

I was pretty sure the guy on the Hills Bros. coffee can was in love with me. Because the way I had been sleeping—or not sleeping, as the case might be—I am pretty sure I had been keeping him in business the past few months.

Gray daylight slithered through the windows and slider doors by the time I wandered downstairs in my Supergirl T-shirt and started the coffee brewing. I hadn't gone back to sleep, partially because of the horrible nightmare I'd experienced and partially because Puddin' Head snores like a bastard. You should have seen the pissed-off cat eye he'd given me when I startled awake that way, too. He'd have done Martha Stewart proud.

My nerves still felt as rattled as a dancing skeleton, not just because of the nightmare but because of what something deep in my mind was telling me the nightmare meant. That it wasn't just a dream. That it was some sort of message and some sort of warning. And some sort of clue.

Dammit, sometimes I wished Evil just came out with things instead of getting off so much on the game.

Bodies burning. Rats. Demon girls. Patricia. Arly in chains. A children's nursery rhyme.

I shivered, getting a good idea now of where things were going, though I wasn't sure if they gave me any clue as to where Arly was being held.

My hand absently went to the locket at my throat and for some reason I felt a fraction calmer.

"Pat..." I whispered. Was she dead? Was she trying to reach me? Was something preventing her from fully materializing or telling me outright what I needed to know?

One thing I had learned was the supernatural didn't work that way. It worked in partials and symbols and pee-in-your-panties warnings. And lucky Arly and me, we were somehow "special"; at least that's the way Lansing had put it. I bet special didn't always keep you from getting killed. Ask Joan of Arc.

While waiting for the coffee to finish brewing, I grabbed the remote and clicked on the tube. I probably shouldn't have. A reporter, some chick with frizzy red hair and a my-crap-doesn't-stink attitude, was interviewing another doctor at New Salem Memorial:

"...appears to be a mutation of the Bubonic Plague, but it is not responding to any conventional treatments."

"So, you're saying this has the potential to spread throughout New Salem, become an epidemic?" the reporter asked. Damned if there wasn't a prissy little smirk on her lips. She loved this kind of crap. It was drama, dammit, and she was Lois frickin' Lane.

"We don't want to start a panic, but we are looking at a possible quarantine—"

Quarantine? The word made my stomach drop. The memory of the sign nailed to the building in my dream came back to me. I clicked off the TV, shuddering, wishing more than ever I hadn't turned it on. But avoiding it would not help and it was nothing I wasn't putting together in the dark recesses of my mind anyway. Quarantine. Bubonic plague. Freakin' great.

I tossed the remote on the couch, then went to the kitchen and grabbed the coffee pot and a mug that said, "My Cat Thinks He Owns Me" on its front. I took the whole pot upstairs. I was going to need it.

When I walked into my room, my big yellow squatter was still languishing on his corner of the bed. He gave me the hairy cat eye, like I was bothering him or something by just walking into my own bedroom, then went back to sleep. Again with the snoring. Ugh.

I set my mug on the small table in the corner that held my computer, poured myself a cup and set the pot down beside it. With a sigh, I fired up my computer and wished I was back in Kansas.

Dammit, things had been so much easier when I was a kid. Before my parents died and my sister was taken, I mean. I wished I could go back to having little girl dreams and innocent days. It would be so much easier than...*this.*

I know, when you're a kid, you can't wait to grow up. And children had their share of fears—the bully, how to get out of eating something your mom cooked for supper you didn't like, and were you going to miss your favorite TV show. Seems like silly stuff when you look back, especially with the litany of adult worries that start at puberty. But at least when you're a child you don't dwell on them so constantly. You can still forget your troubles and hide yourself in your little girl fantasies and dolls and games.

Ring-a-ring-of-roses...

Well, maybe not *that* game.

I sighed again. It was all relative, I suppose. And you played the cards you'd been dealt, even if the dealer was the Devil.

The computer beeped and the flat screen told me Windows had loaded. I clicked my Internet icon and brought up Cloogle.

After downing a gulp of coffee, I typed *Ring Around the Rosie* into the search box, noticing my hands were shaking a bit.

It took me only a few minutes to learn the rhyme had a number of variations related to region, though the tune remained the same.

And almost as quickly I learned it had an urban legend attached to it.

According to the 20th century interpretation the rhyme related to the Black Plague.

Ring around the rosie
Pocketful of posies
Ashes, ashes
We all fall down...

The first line referred to the red rings that appeared on victims' faces. The second indicated the sweet smelling flowers stuffed in the unfortunates' pockets to cover the odor of the erupting sores or ward off illness. Ashes, ashes originally was *atishu, atishu,* pertaining to the sound of sneezing, but apparently my demon girl was a bit more literal than that. The last line…well, that's obvious.

I spent another half hour researching the Bubonic Plague, not much liking what I found and how it mimicked the points in my dream and what the news was reporting in town. A plague. Here in New Salem. A demon girl. A demonic harbinger of a dreadful event or the direct cause of it?

"Jesus, that's just soooo Old World," I whispered without any humor. But Evil stuck with what worked, I guess. Or what they thought worked, since we usually ended up kicking their ass in the end. But you had to give Evil props for creating unrest and fear. Maybe that's what sustained It until It achieved Its final end.

And if Evil couldn't directly kill Arly, as Genie Lansing had once told him, was It hoping to use him for something associated with the plague? Or something deeper than that?

Some things suddenly made deadly sense while other things did not. And nothing about it told me where to find him.

I closed out of the search engine and leaned back in my chair, about to switch off the computer. The screen suddenly went black.

I was about to let out a curse, then remembered the Blue Screen was the one to worry about if something was wrong with your machinery. I should have let the curse fly anyway. Because an instant later the black screen reminded me there were evils worse than Microsoft.

My name in dark red letters flashed in the center of the ebony screen. It vanished almost as suddenly as it had come.

Then another name blinked in its place.

Praetallious.

In a moment of panic I couldn't really explain, I jabbed the off button. But the name didn't go away. It kept blinking on the screen and a little girl's laughter suddenly echoed from everywhere in my bedroom.

I let out a startled yip and noticed Puddin' Head jumping off the bed. Evil didn't frighten him, it just annoyed him. I could tell by the put-out way he sauntered from the room. Had he been capable of uttering obscenities he would have.

Then the laughter stopped and the name vanished from the screen, as if the laughter had taken it.

"Patricia?" I asked, getting out of my chair. "Are you here?"

Everything became suddenly far too silent, though for the quickest of heartbeats I swore I heard my name whispered by a little girl.

TWENTY-SEVEN

Hi Ho, Hi Ho, it's Off to Church We Go...

The day had gotten even more gray by the time I showered, pulled my hair back into a ponytail and got my heart out of my throat. I pulled on a pair of jeans and a blue sweater, made sure Puddin' Head's dish was full—because, God knew, I'd hear about it later if I forgot to make sure His Majesty went an hour or two without chow—then grabbed my backpack and headed out.

I had some pieces, now, enough to form a theory about what Little Miss Demonic was up to, if not what it had to do with Arly or where he'd vanished to. I think Arly would have been proud of me, because at least I had an idea where to go next to follow up on what he'd been trying to tell me, and what Patricia had been trying to warn me about. Of course, if I was wrong, I was going to feel pretty let down, but I needed something to focus on. I need something to feel like I was moving forward instead of standing still.

I had a name: Praetallious. I wasn't positive but I was betting it was either that little demon girl or somehow connected to her and the outbreak of the mysterious illness sending the good people of New Salem to the hospital. I also had decided maybe Arly's words, "Saint" and "Patricia" might be linked, though I wasn't exactly sure how there, either. That gave me two options.

After tossing my backpack onto the car seat and climbing in behind the wheel, I pulled the Beretta's door shut. Grabbing my backpack again, I fished out my cell phone and went for my first option, which I figured might be the quickest of the two. Ms. Pixie Sticks was hiding something; I had become more and more certain of that. She had told me just enough to keep me on a path, though for what reason I had no clue. She wanted me to know about that locket without wanting to tell me—you get what I mean? But it was bad enough Evil was into the whole cloak and dagger thing. I had decided the imp crushing on my man wasn't going to get away with it, too.

I had programmed the museum's number into my cell and it took two rings for that snotty receptionist to answer. I knew it was her immediately because her tone matched her attitude and I swore she somehow knew it was me before I even said a word.

"I need to talk to Genie Lansing," I said. Somehow, in my mind's eye, I knew the little bitch was smirking when she replied:

"*Ms.* Lansing is not available at the moment, Miss Everson."

Well, that confirmed she knew who I was. I should have been surprised but I wasn't. Lansing had something indefinably peculiar about her, so why not Little Miss Retro Punk?

"She better make herself available," I said, in no mood to have my chain jerked.

That resulted in three minutes of arguing and a not-so-pleasant name referencing the girl's breeding getting past my lips. Like I have said, being a stripper, you get used to dealing with troublesome people, but honestly my nerves were just shot all to hell and I had had it up to my assets with getting nowhere. I swear if she had been standing in front of me I would have poked a finger in her eye and twisted her ear off.

The result was me telling her I would be calling back in an hour or two and *Ms.* Frickin' Lansing better have made herself available by that time or I was going to go all Stripper on her ass, which is a lot like going postal only with scratching and hair pulling.

I jammed my cell back into my backpack, the anger surging through my veins chasing away some of the worry and fear for the time being.

I started the car and backed out of my spot, left with my second idea, one that made me a bit nervous, though it probably shouldn't have.

It had been a lifetime since I set foot in a church. I have vague memories of my parents taking my sister and me to a Methodist one, I think, but let's face it, strippers and churches are a bit like oil and water. Oh, I know some dancers who attend. I have a feeling they have some idea it makes them less likely to be dropped down the no zip code chute after they die. Maybe they want forgiveness. Me, I don't need forgiveness, at least not for stripping, because I don't feel guilty about it and I am pretty sure God has seen me naked. And I figure after dealing with Ficatier and her traveling witch band the Big Guy erased any tab I might have rung up. At least that's what I tell myself. And while I personally figure stripping isn't a sin, if it does somehow end up on the list it will have to be pretty low down, considering the things that go on in New Salem.

I am starting to sound wishy-washy, aren't I? Maybe I'm starting to feel that way a bit, too, because the anger was wearing off and the thought of how I was going to broach monkeys, demon girls and Biblical plagues to a Priest so it didn't sound like I was a nutjob just out of Bellevue suddenly made me even more nervous about being in a church than I had been a moment ago.

"Saint" and "Patricia," Arly had said. Those might be two separate things, one referring to my sister, the other to God knew what, but I was taking a leap and combining them, hoping it would lead me somewhere. It was the only thing I had beyond the weird name that had popped onto my computer screen. Saints, I was pretty sure, went with Catholics, so that was my destination.

There was no St. Patricia's in New Salem or any of the surrounding towns—I had checked through the phone book before my shower—so I headed for New Salem's only Catholic listing: St. Luke's. St. Luke's was located midtown, a Burger King on one side and a Taco Bell on the other. That probably made sense to somebody or maybe it saved the church the trouble of haddock suppers.

The church itself was a little over a hundred years old with recently redone white siding. Smallish and if I had to guess I'd say maybe it would hold one- to two-hundred parishioners at the most. If the plague stuff kept up they might have to build an addition, because the demon and disease combination had me thinking about those apocalyptic horror movies where everybody suddenly learns to pray right before kissing their ass goodbye.

I pulled into the parking lot and shut off the car. With a deep breath, I grabbed my backpack and got out, hoping whoever the priest was here he would be in and a lot more talkative than Ms. Genie Lansing. Assuming he didn't think I was a complete loony the moment I brought up demon girls and plagues, of course.

TWENTY-EIGHT

Bless Me for I Have Sinned...a Lot

I was surprised the church wasn't locked, but in New Salem easy access to a place of worship was probably a good thing.

The interior was gloomy, gray light diffusing through the stained glass windows of various Saints. Some kind of odd aroma permeated the place, flowery, but mixed with body odor, varnish and maybe a little bit of flame-broiled hamburger filtering in from the Burger King next door. The hushed heavy silence reminded me of a morgue and my footsteps echoed like the ghosts of mourners marching to a dirge as I walked down the aisle between the pews. I noticed flowers on the altar and something in my stomach dropped. Obviously there'd been a funeral here, or maybe, worse, one was going to take place later in the day. A burst of relief came with the fact that no coffin rested in front of the altar, but I still fought a powerful urge to turn around and walk out. The church was empty, anyway, so leaving the place wouldn't have taken much of a push. I had noticed a building behind the church, which was probably the rectory. The priest might be there—assuming he was on the premises at all—and it passed through my mind I'd likely have to go through another snotty secretary like the one at the museum. Older, of course, but just as annoying, or perhaps more so because she'd had longer to practice.

I've never felt comfortable in a church. It's not because I feel any real guilt over being a stripper, it's just something...

Ok, I'm waffling. I know the reason. It's because my last memory of one was the funeral for my parents. A lot of that day is a blur, but I remember tears. From myself, from Pat, from relatives and friends. Tears that seemed never to stop. The smells, much like the ones I was getting in here now, but mixed with all the mourners' perfume and cologne; the looks on everybody's faces that just made the tears flow harder; the soothing voices that promised it would get better with time…lies supposed to comfort, but lies useless to a child, and lies nevertheless. Things didn't get better; you just learned to live with them. Pain wasn't as acute after a few months or a year, a decade, but it never went away, not totally. It lived deep inside, aching, burning, ready to flare up at a sight or sound or scent that triggered a memory, good or bad, of how you'd lost someone that meant so much. Someones, in my case. Both parents. And eventually my sister, too.

I forced myself to stop thinking about it because tears were welling again and right now I couldn't let that get in the way. I spent enough nights missing my folks, my sister, the things that could have been but never were. Now, I needed to focus on Arly and the things that, if I found him, might be.

"Miss?"

"Jesus!" I blurted, nearly coming out of my skin at the voice that had come from behind me. I spun to see a man in a collar standing about five feet away. He was a hell of a lot younger than I expected a priest to be, maybe forty, with bright blue eyes and…damn, he was a priest, I reminded myself. But I didn't know they came good-looking.

"More like His second or third in command," he said. I think it was a joke, but I had all I could do to stop from shuddering with nerves.

"Sorry," I said. "You startled me."

He gave me a strange smile. "I was looking out one of the rectory windows when you drove up. I saw you enter the church. I didn't mean to scare you."

I felt like saying scaring me didn't take a hell of a lot at this point. And it dawned on me I still had no real decent way of broaching my subject without sounding like a first class fruit loop.

"I, uh…" Oh, that was brilliant. Being at a loss for words normally wasn't a problem for me, but damned if I could more than stutter. I wished to hell he was old and had those creepy-crawly white eyebrows I expected on priests. I mean, priests were s'posed to be old and…I dunno, fatherly or something.

"Confession isn't for a few hours…" he said.

Hmmph. I really wasn't sure whether that was a joke. He wasn't laughing. Or smiling. His tone wasn't particularly revealing, either. Did he think I needed to confess something?

"I not Catholic," I said. More brilliance. I was really going to have to work on the clever repartee if I was going to keep helping out Arly. "I've got nothing to confess." I added that like I felt guilty or something. Not sure why.

"Oh, no?"

Ok, this time he had an expression and I really didn't care a lot for it. It reminded me of Genie Lansing somehow.

I noticed another thing, too. A stripper friend of mine at the Lagoon had insisted all priests were gay. I knew better, but it had stuck in my mind. This guy? Nuh-uh. Collar or no, his peepers took a crawl over my sweater and planted a flag on Mounts Chloe.

"You sure you're not Episcopalian?" I asked, trying to joke it off, but just sounding like an idiot.

"I don't know what you mean, Miss...?"

"Everson. Chloe Everson."

"Miss Everson..." He looked at me then like he knew me. I wondered why.

"I came here for some information, actually." I figured I better just come out with it.

He nodded, leaned a hip against a pew. "Is this a faith matter?"

"Umm...some might call it that, but it's more like a missing persons matter."

His brow crinkled. "You're not with the police."

He said it like he knew it as a fact. "I am helping them out." Ah, the brilliance just kept coming. Jeez, this was making dealing with pawing drunks look easy. "A friend of mine, he...he's missing and the police haven't been able to find any trace of him."

"What makes you think I can help?"

Ok, now we were going to get to the screwy part and I felt like bolting out of the church and finding another way to go about this. But I couldn't. If there was any chance at all this might lead to a clue to where Arly was being held, I had to risk it.

"Look, you're gonna think I'm nuts..." Out with it, I figured. Straight up, stirred not shaken. "But my friend has been *taken*..."

Up went his eyebrow. "Taken?"

"Please, don't ask me to explain it because it won't make sense."

He laughed and I wasn't sure whether it was at me. "This is New Salem."

And just like that I felt a surge of relief. I hadn't expected it, but something in his last statement had told me he might have seen things, here in this town, things that weren't exactly Godly.

"Have you ever heard the name Praetallious?"

His expression didn't change and he shook his head. "I'm afraid not. Does he have something to do with your missing friend?"

I nodded. "I'm betting he—" or "it", I wanted to say, but refrained—"does."

"Who is this Praetallious? Where did you hear the name?"

"You wouldn't believe me." I wrapped my arms across my chest. I normally didn't have any problem with guys taking a peek at my cleavage, but a good-looking young priest, well, I didn't really need to get that close to pissing off the Big Guy, not in my present standing with the supernatural.

Another laugh, short, but not mocking. "Try me."

"It appeared on my computer screen. But it's not the only strange thing that has been appearing to me lately."

He nodded, no patronizing look in his eyes, which were thankfully off my chest. "And these things appearing…they have something to do with your missing friend, too?"

"I think they do. I've seen things…" I don't quite know why I was telling him that. It only made me sound crazy. "But I was hoping you might know the name because…well, because…" Oh, crap, how was I going to say Arly and a demon girl had appeared to me in a dream and in glass and said something about a saint?

"We've all seen things in New Salem, Miss Everson. Most won't admit it, or deal with it, but that doesn't mean those things aren't…real."

I peered at him, studying his face and saw something in his eyes, some kind of sadness or something. I wasn't entirely certain what it was, I guess. But it wasn't pleasant.

"You know, don't you?"

He shrugged. "I *don't* know, Miss Everson. But I suspect. And I suspect worse is to come, but…well, men of the cloth are always raving about that sort of thing, aren't they? Maybe too much so, to the point where few take it serious or the ones who do are labeled as nuts. And frankly some of them are. They'll accept anything that smacks of doom and gloom because their psyche demands it of them. And therein lies Evil's greatest strength."

Well, blow me down, as Popeye says. This priest had eaten his spinach. He even managed to say that without sounding like a movie cliché, no matter what it sounds like.

But a thought sobered me: If he didn't know the name, then I had probably wasted my time coming here and that meant no clue to where Arly might be.

"Is there a Saint Patricia?" I asked, not sure where else to go with my questions. I had seriously hoped against hope Praetallious was some sort of Catholic boogeyman and that Father Scope-My-Boobs would know the name, and that it would lead me where I wanted to go.

He shook his head. "Not that I am aware of. But we've got a lot of Saints." He tried a smile but it wasn't cute or comfortable anymore. I could see worry in his eyes and I had brought that to the front by coming here. I suddenly felt like the stripper harbinger of doom.

I knew he was too young to have been a priest here when my sister and I were separated, but I asked anyway, "Did you ever meet a Patricia Everson?"

Another shake of the head and my hopes plunged like a barrel going over Niagara Falls.

"But I met a Sister Patricia once. She was with us briefly at St. Bosco's"

"Saint Bosco?" I almost laughed but it was a nervous reaction. "You named a Saint after chocolate?"

"It seemed better than naming him after broccoli. At least to get the kids into church."

This time he was joking and it relieved my disappointment only a fraction.

"Where is this St. Bosco's?" I asked. I hadn't seen it in the phone-book and this Sister Patricia was probably no relation to my sister, Pat, but Evil had a thing about funny coincidences.

"It's at the outskirts of New Salem. Doesn't belong to the church anymore, though. They sold it off and nothing was ever done with it. Probably falling in by now."

"Do you know who bought it?" I asked.

"I believe it was a former public servant or something, a woman."

My stomach headed south. "Not a district attorney…"

His brow crinkled. "Might have been."

"A black woman, by any chance?" My stomach just kept right on dropping.

He nodded and I felt sick. "I believe so. I think she talked about renovating it and moving her offices there. Not sure what happened to her or why she didn't."

I could have told him. Because a name locked in my mind, a name I didn't want there. Ficatier. Angelique Ficatier.

"Why did the church sell the building? That doesn't happen very often, does it?"

"Officially, it was too expensive to keep up. It was an old stone and brick building, drafty and needed a great deal of renovation. Its fellowship was small and it couldn't support itself. A money drain for the church at a time of widespread parish consolidation."

I could see it in his eyes: that wasn't the real story. "And unofficially?"

He looked away, his face going distant as he peered at the crucifix suspended above the altar. "Unofficially, the place was said to be haunted, built originally on a 'dark spot', one of a number of them in this town, if you are familiar with some of New Salem's egregious history. Accidents occurred with increasing regularity and severity; there was even the death of a young nun....Something about the place wasn't...right. An exorcism didn't stop whatever was occurring, so the church deemed it a loss."

"They ran?"

He nodded, disappointment on his face. "It amounts to that, I suppose."

"That makes me feel a whole lot more confident about the church's help with what you said might be coming."

"It shouldn't..." he said.

I wanted to tell him I was being sarcastic but his mood had become very peculiar, somber. There was more to him than met the eye but I suddenly didn't have the time to dig it out. My mind had leaped to connections. Sister Patricia. A haunted church purchased by the former D.A., a woman who had headed a band of renegade Salem witches intent on bringing a demon back into this world. Too many coincidences for my taste and in that vision I had seen of Arly in the glass he had been shackled to something. An old stone and brick church...shackles...I might have said a prayer, then, or dropped a hundred in the collection plate because a wave of hope washed over me.

"I need directions to this church." I said it with such seriousness he took a step back.

"Why?" he asked, and I really had no desire to tell him.

"I can find the information elsewhere, I'm sure, Father, but I've learned a lot about the workings of the 'other side', for lack of a better name. They like games. They like coincidence and taunts. And right now I've got a hell of gut feeling I've just been given the Rosetta Stone for translating this Praetallious' sense of the ironic."

The look on his face said he didn't really like what I was telling him but that he knew I was right and would find the address easy enough. He also realized it was important and a few minutes either way might be crucial. He gave me the location.

"Thank you, Father…?" It dawned on me I hadn't gotten his name.

"Lansing," he said with an odd little smile.

Lansing? You had to be freakin' kidding me. That would explain some of the feeling I had that he might know me. "Do you have a sister or female cousin or something?"

His smile twitched. "No, I'm an only child and my family…are all dead."

I got the distinct impression that he was leaving out something but I had no time to play twenty questions with him at the moment. I nodded, then started to hurry down the aisle.

"Miss Everson?" he called out, and I paused.

"Yes, Father?" I didn't turn to look back at him.

"What you do, it's a sin, you know…"

How the hell did he even know what…and then it dawned on me. He had been staring at my boobs because he had been to the Lagoon.

"If that's the case, then isn't watching it a sin, too?" I said it without malice or sarcasm. I heard him utter a short laugh.

"We all have our demons…"

"You don't even know…" I said, with a nervous titter. "But I don't believe it's a sin, Father. I believe it's a gift and God's seen me naked a whole lot more times than you have." I turned and winked at him. Now I was in *my* element.

His face got this really serious look of a doctor telling a patient their arm had just dropped off. "All I mean is don't let sin make you vulnerable. What's coming…they take advantage of anything…even with the 'special' ones."

Special ones. Again he reminded me of that other Lansing, at least the things she said. I would have questioned him more about that, but I had to find St. Bosco's and stumble blindly into the Devil's Playground the way I always did.

I only hoped this wasn't the time that got me killed.

TWENTY-NINE

Arrival

The fact that I had no idea what I was going to do if I found Arly and that demon girl at St. Bosco's should have given me pause.

But it didn't.

I think I told you Arly calls me impulsive, that I tend to charge into things without spending a lot of time thinking about them beforehand. This was going to be another one of those times.

Even so, I figured I might try taking a couple precautions, though what good they would do was debatable.

As I drove toward the church, which lay just at the outskirts of New Salem in a heavily wooded area, I tried to keep my foot from stomping the accelerator and sending the Beretta along the backwoods street at a hundred miles an hour. The gray sky had begun to spit rain and the road was just at that greasy point before the pavement got totally soaked. An accident or a speeding ticket would have put a serious crimp in my timing, so I kept my speed a little above the limit—I heard they don't stop you for five miles over, is that true? Seems like I should have known that dating an ex-cop and being friends with a present one.

A memory suddenly came to me of the first time I had given Arly a ride home in this car. I had scared the hell out of him. I almost laughed at the thought but the sobering notion that there was still plenty of hell left to go around brought me back to present.

I had to pry one of my white hands off the steering wheel to fish in the pocket of my backpack on the passenger seat. I located my cell phone.

Two precautions, I said? More like just potential backup in case what I felt in my gut came to be.

I flipped open the phone and with my thumb hit the button for the museum.

Genie Lansing was more than she let on, and I felt certain she knew more, far more, than she was telling. She wasn't about to spill it outright, but if it had something to do with St. Bosco's or my sister, I might need her in some way. Who she was—or maybe *what* she was, the thought came to me—was a mystery, and getting to be more of one all the time in my book, but while she annoyed the hell out of me I didn't get a feeling of evil from her. I got a feeling of…well, I wasn't sure what it was, maybe neutrality or something, or leaning towards Good.

The snotty little receptionist answered again and I stifled a groan.

"I want Lansing this time," I said with as much authority as I could muster, given the fact my heart was throbbing in my throat and my legs were syrupy.

"She's not—"

"Yeah, yeah, available. Give her to me anyway." I was in no mood for a run-around.

"I'm sorry," the little punkass said. "She's not available…"

"We established that, as well as the fact I don't give a damn." One thing I appreciated about my temper: it chased away some of the fear. "You tell her I don't know what the hell her game is but I'm on my way to St. Bosco's right now and if she's got anything on her mind about Arlo Grimm and what's going on in New Salem she better get her little pixie ass over there or next time it won't be Curious Skull-face's bones in a box."

I thought that sounded pretty tough, but it was probably just melo-dramatic and I don't think it impressed the punky receptionist in the least.

In fact, I was sure of it because I heard a click. The stupid bitch had hung up on me.

I let out a frustrated yell and refrained from hurling the phone against the windshield. Instead, I hit another programmed number and waited four rings.

"Dammit!" I said, getting Sturdevant's voicemail. I hate voicemail. I especially hated it right now when I needed him, though I still wasn't sure what he could do. It occurred to me I might just get us both killed, but a selfish fear made me leave him a message telling him I thought I had a lead to Arly and Little Miss Demonic and was headed to a haunted church to do something about it.

"Looks like I do this alone…" I muttered.

After stuffing the phone back into my backpack, I concentrated on the road ahead. Rain started coming down a bit harder and I had to speed up the wipers.

Couldn't the frickin' sun ever be shining when you confronted Evil? I asked myself, pretty much knowing the answer. Evil not only liked the game, it liked the trappings. Evil liked to set the mood, play on the dark and depressive. It shunned sunlight and openness.

"Well, crap," was all I could think of saying.

I started to wonder if Evil had heard me mocking its tactics because the rain actually let up by the time I reached the church. I pulled the car to the opposite side of the deserted street, took another deep breath and let it out, then shut off the engine. I touched the bulge of the locket beneath my sweater, hoping Lansing was right about it being protective, then got out of the car.

After easing the door shut—like Evil, if it were here, didn't already know I was coming and making as little noise as possible closing a car door would do any good—I peered across the street at the church. No other buildings were on the street except the decrepit stone and brick building built in ugly Gothic lines and another smaller stone structure behind it that I assumed was the Rectory. Last fall's decaying brown leaves and scrabbly patches of brush littered the grounds. A wooden walkway leading to the church was in shambles, boards rotting, paint peeling. A number of the stained glass windows had been taken out, probably by delinquents with rocks, but I thought I saw some kind of glow flickering from within and the feeling in my gut that this was where I would find Arly and the demon girl strengthened. Flickering is never good, let me tell you, unless you're in a bathroom with a glass of wine and the scent of lavender candles filling the air.

But no lavender here, just the odor of rot and decay and dark things. I shivered, despite my struggle to hold my nerves together.

"Arly, dammit, you better be alive…"

I started across the street, telling myself that if he wasn't no power in Hell was going to keep me from tearing apart that demon mockery of my sister.

THIRTY

Say Twenty Hail Chloes…then Run Like Hell

I was right about flickering. Not being a good sign, I mean. Because as I entered St. Bosco's, torches in wall sconces illuminated a room in a dreadful state of disrepair, far more decrepit than the church's exterior and grounds. But that was secondary to the fact that no churches I knew of used torches anymore. Even the Catholics had entered the 21st Century—well, at least in respect to using electricity—so the feeling in my gut that this was where I would find the answer to Arly's disappearance became a chilling certainty.

The huge wooden door—it reminded me of a dungeon door, but I quickly suppressed that notion—was unlocked. Second church today, I thought, only this time I was certain it was open for a far more…I wanted to say "dark" but settled for "baiting" reason. Whatever that thing masquerading as my sister was, it knew I was coming, had probably known all along that I would find this place, find Arly, and now it was challenging me to step up to the plate.

Great. I didn't have any kind of weapon. I knew damn little about demons other than what I'd been forced to learn after the Sisters of the Snake nearly killed me, and I wasn't even Catholic, so an exorcism or mumbo jumbo from some horror movie wasn't going to save my ass *or* Arly's. I was a stripper; what was I going to do? Tassel the demon to death?

I shivered, despite myself, partly from a sense of helplessness as the reality set in that I had blundered into yet another situation without a plan and because the damned dungeonlike door shrieked on rusty hinges as I pushed it open.

Like I said, the jittering light from the torches showed me a church interior long fallen into disuse and probably the victim of more than a few vandals. A stray thought made me wonder if those vandals had made it out alive and my gaze scanned the debris-strewn floor for any signs of old bones. Fortunately I saw none, but that was only a mild relief.

The flame light cavorted with shadow over the stone walls and remains of stained glass windows, like frightened black and gold ghosts offering a warning they knew I would ignore. Most of the pews had been over-turned, many splintered—damn, if I had been facing a vampire I would have been all set; plenty of stakes around. No such luck. Years worth of fast food bags and containers littered the stone-tiled aisle. Many of the tiles were chipped or pried up completely. Old church bulletins, yellowed and torn, lay scattered about. A decayed odor of old garbage and something I didn't care to dwell on made my stomach revolt. I heard skittering noises, which thrilled me not in the least, because I knew rodents or roaches had made the place their home.

Ring-a-ring of roses...

Oh, crap. Rodents. Rats. Plague. Just what the doctor ordered.

I was thankful I couldn't see them, but as I started down the aisle, my legs shaking as bad as the first day I had removed my top for a crowd of drunken leering men, I was ready to come out of my skin the moment anything jumped out in front of me.

Maybe you're not cut out for this...

The thought did me little good, because right now I didn't have a choice. Maybe I never had one. Maybe something had chosen both Arly *and* me for this...what? Mission? Could I call it that? That's as good a word as any, I s'pose. Maybe something had selected us for this mission and we had no choice but to see it through.

Or die.

Arly's special. You're special...that's why you have the locket...

That's what Lansing had indicated, right? But right now I didn't feel very special. I felt vulnerable and alone and forced onward only by a fact I had realized before that now came to a head: I loved Arly more than I loved my own life and would be willing to sacrifice that life to get him back safe. He would have done the same thing for me, in fact, had risked his life times over against Ficatier to do just that.

I squeezed my tail between my legs and continued down the aisle.

"Where are you?" I yelled. "Praetallious or whatever the hell your name is? Where's Arly? What have you done with him?"

Silence. Mostly. The damn skittering again, as if leaves, driven by a ghost wind, were scratching across a stone floor.

Another shiver, stronger this time, went through me. I wrapped my arms about myself.

Ashes, ashes...

"I know you're here somewhere. You knew I'd find this place." My yelling echoed off the stones walls, for a fraction of a thought glazed with the laugh of a little girl.

I was right. Some*thing* was here.

"Patricia?" I yelled. "Is that you?"

I knew it wasn't, couldn't be. It had to be some kind of Evil trick. Evil was big on tricks. And those tricks more often than not worked because Evil knew how to get at what you desired or trusted most. Evil used your Good against you. Evil got off on that and I was determined not to let it.

"You can't have Arly, you know that! You can't have me. You're wasting your time...so just give up now or..."

Or what? Oh, crap on a cracker, I had nothing. What was I going to do, threaten to bump and grind Evil out of New Salem? I really should have been cop instead of a dancer.

You can't have him...

The voice came from everywhere yet nowhere, the vaguest of whispers, tainted with a sickening feeling of dread that crawled up from the depths of my own mind.

"Where are you?" I yelled, working at getting my anger up to cover the fear.

She's coming back...

What? She? Patricia? Who?

Then the feeling faded, suddenly, as if some other...*force?* dampened it temporarily.

Even so, I let out a bleat of fear as something moved on the altar and startled the living hell out of me.

THIRTY-ONE

Genie Out of the Bottle

"Jesus!" I blurted, feeling a little like a fool, but I think I mentioned my nerves felt as tight as one of my G-strings.

On the altar, Genie Lansing gave me that smug little smile of hers and took the three steps down to the aisle floor. I got the impression she didn't want to stay on altar because she gave it a backward glance and a hint of disgust replaced the smugness. I couldn't blame her. Garbage littered the altar area and the crucifix was hanging upside down. I noticed plenty of feces too, probably from rats.

Ms. Pixie Sticks leaned a hand on the back of a pew, her plastic bracelets rattling. "I don't think we have any worries about Jesus showing up in this place..."

It struck me as an odd thing to say. I think she was making a joke, but wasn't entirely certain and this didn't seem the time for one. "It *is* a church..." Not sure my own statement sounded a whole lot brighter but I was still trying to make myself stop shaking.

"It *was* a church..." She glanced at the altar again. "Now...now it's something else."

"Just how the hell did you come to be here?"

"There's a back door."

I shook my head. "That's not what I meant, though seems like I would have heard you come in that way." I glanced to either side of the altar. A door lay to each side, one of them open. She could have come in that way, I suppose, but still...

She shrugged. And it annoyed me. In fact, everything about her still annoyed me; that hadn't changed since our first meeting.

"You called my assistant." She said it like that answered every-thing, or she *wanted* it to answer everything. I wasn't much in the mood for letting her off the hook.

"No, I just called before I reached here. There's no way you could have gotten here from the museum that fast."

She gave me a patronizing smile. "You're not the only one with a cell phone, Miss Everson. My assistant called and told me to meet you here. I was only a few streets away."

"Harassing lawn gnomes, I take it?" My sarcasm was taking over and getting rid of some of the effects of the jolt I had taken.

"I don't understand."

I wasn't surprised, but as I glanced over her flower-print skirt and loose blue top I didn't notice any pockets for a cell phone. She could have left it in her car, I guess, but something just didn't feel right about the way she had…what? Appeared, was the word I wanted to use. It was like she wasn't there one moment and the next…

My attention had been diverted by the whispers I heard, but I couldn't make myself accept her explanation totally.

"When I was leaving the museum, I saw a monkey go into your of-fice. I went after him, but the room was empty. You couldn't have got-ten out of that office without me seeing you. I was right there in the hall."

Her smile wasn't quite as smug this time. "I'm sure you were overwrought, mistaken."

"Oh!" My blood started racing and the urge to pop her one became nearly overwhelming. "Don't even!"

"Miss Everson, please. We have more important matters to discuss than—"

M-S Pixie Sticks was really pissing me off. I'd had it up to here with Evil's little tricks and wasn't about to take them from her.

"Look, just who the hell are you really, Ms. Lansing? I better start getting some answers out of you because my last nerve is about to snap and if it does you're going to need to pry my foot out of your lit-tle white ass."

I thought it sounded tough but she gave me a look with her misty marble eyes that said I couldn't have done anything to her had I tried. I felt an urge to take backward step but held my ground.

If she had even intended on replying any response was stifled by a sudden scurrying from the right side of the altar. A monkey scampered out of the open door and up to Genie Lansing. The little sucker grabbed hold of her skirt and climbed his way to her shoulder.

I knew that frickin' monkey; he was the same one who had shown up at my apartment in the dead of night. I touched the locket beneath my sweater as his beady little eyes focused on me. Genie Lansing stroked his tail, let him wrap it about her fingertip. He started doing that creepy monkey thing with his forehead and I realized their expressions were almost exactly the same. And they say dogs and owners start to look alike.

"Curious Skullface belongs to you, doesn't he?" I had figured it out already; I just wanted to hear her admit it.

"I like to call him Bob." She offered a wan smile and Bob chittered. I think it was a chitter. It might have been the monkey equivalent of "piss off."

"And those bones in the box? Were those his?" I ducked my chin at the furry ugly.

The monkey let out a shriek that could have peeled paint.

"He's sensitive about that," Genie Lansing said. The monkey began to pick through her white-blonde hair.

"He should be, but you didn't answer my question."

"Yes, those were his. It's..." She paused, as if searching for a way to put me off again. "Complicated."

"I bet it is, seeing as how he's sitting on your shoulder and bones in a box at the same time. If this weren't New Salem..."

Lansing nodded, face a bit more somber now. "The bones were a warning to you, and to me."

I nodded. I had figured that out, too. She probably thought I was stupid, probably figured all women who stripped for a living were stupid. Condescending little bitch. "I understand why I'd be warned off, but why you?"

She took a few steps into the aisle, turned away from me. I wasn't sure for a moment that she wasn't just going to leave. But then she turned, peered directly at me, with something in those misty marble eyes I hadn't seen before: a hint of worry.

"These things have repercussions, Miss Everson. I'm not supposed to...help. None of us are."

"Who's none of us? You and...?"

"I think you know the answer to that."

Pat. She meant Pat. Pat wasn't supposed to help, but somehow she had tried. And the demon was overriding her.

I wanted to press her further on that, and on her own role, but I had come here to find Arly and confront that apparition that looked like my sister. "Who or what is Praetallious?" I asked instead.

"You already know."

"That's not a lot of help..." But then it dawned on me. She was right. "The little girl demon, the one that looks little Pat..."

"It's not a little girl. Praetallious appears as a manifestation of something in your deepest thoughts. In this case, he's chosen your sister."

"Why?"

"What do you want most, Miss Everson? Besides Alro Grimm, who do you miss in your deepest soul?"

I nodded. "My sister."

Evil uses whatever makes you most vulnerable..." She paused, as if she were listening to something somewhere else. Her eyes narrowed. "I am forbidden to say more."

"Forbidden by whom?" I knew she wasn't going to answer that. Even if she had it wouldn't have mattered because I heard something, then. It came low, just at the edge of my hearing: the distant rattling of a chain.

"Arly!" I blurted and I could tell by the sudden widening of Lansing's eyes she had thought—or knew?—the same thing.

My gaze went to the second door, the one still closed on the left side of the altar. The sound had come from behind that door, I was damn near certain. I rushed over to it and grabbed the glass handle. The knob wouldn't budge. They lock one damn door in the whole church and this was it?

It made me more certain than ever I was right about Arly being on the other side.

I glanced back at Lansing, half expecting her to have vanished, but she had come up behind me. Curious Bob had jumped onto a pew and was giving me the monkey eye.

"It's locked," I said, stating the obvious.

"Let me try." Lansing shoved in front of me and gripped the handle. I couldn't quite see what she was doing but I heard clink from the other side, like a key dropping out of a lock and onto a stone floor. She pushed the door open.

"That door was locked." My brow furrowed. "You couldn't have…"

"You loosened it," she said, glancing at me with a big frickin' lie written all over her prissy little face. "The key jiggled loose on the other side."

I didn't believe her but now wasn't really the time to argue about it. From behind the door I could see torch light flickering along a stone stairway that spiraled downward. I pushed past her, my tendency to rush headlong into things getting the better of me.

THIRTY-TWO

Follow the Devil Brick Road

I took a few steps downward, then paused, a wave of apprehension washing through me. What if Arly was at the end of wherever this stairway led…more to the point, what if he was dead and something else had rattled the chain to lure me down here?

"He's not dead…" Lansing said behind me and I turned to look back at her, my surprise showing on my face.

"How did you know what I was—"

Pixie Sticks shrugged. "Lucky guess."

Lying again, and I got the strange notion she was somehow rummaging around in my mind. That just made me comfortable as all hell.

"How can you be so sure they didn't kill him?" I wasn't really positive I wanted the answer to that, because if it made no sense to me I was only going to get more worried that something terrible had happened to him since he'd appeared to me in my dream. Like whatever had happened wasn't already terrible enough.

"They need him." She said it like I should have already known the answer—ok, I probably did, he was special and all that, but that arrogant edge to her tone just pissed me off further, as did everything else about M-S Lansing.

"For what?" I took a step downward. The steps were made of stone, as were the walls. Torches in sconces spaced at uneven intervals gave the stairwell a dungeonlike creepy atmosphere that rode my nerves.

"Same thing Ficatier needed him for."

She was answering without really answering and that was frickin' annoying.

"Can't you just give me a straight explanation?" A shard of anger got into my voice but I doubt she was intimidated. She might have been a bitch but I had a feeling damn little scared her. And right now just about everything was scaring me. "Czcarabus and Ficatier are both dead, gone to Hell or wherever naughty demons and their concubines go."

"Hell has an open door policy."

I paused again and turned back to her, exasperation narrowing my eyes and forcing a sigh from my lips. "Please…"

I think she enjoyed my frustration because that damn little smile was back. "When Arlo Grimm destroyed Ficatier and her demon, he didn't really destroy them. He merely sent them to what amounts to a confinement, like sending a killer to prison for life."

"Except in this case it's supposed to be eternity."

"Eternity is a long time."

Ok, that smile had to go. "That's the stupidest thing you've said so far."

Yup, smile gone. I'd gotten under her skin. Kudos to me.

"Eternity is not the problem. Prisoners escape jail. That happens with demons and witches such as Ficatier, too."

"Arlo cut off her head. That seems like more like getting the death penalty."

She shrugged and by the glint in her eyes I could tell it wasn't like getting the death penalty; it was more like having a tooth extracted.

"There is only one permanent solution."

"And that would be?" I started downward again, trying to suppress my growing mixture of fear and irritation.

"Sending them to the Vanished Place."

"The what, now?" I made a mental note that Evil wasn't the only thing that enjoyed talking in riddles. Lansing was from the same school, probably head of her class.

"The Vanished Place. The permanent deposition of Evil."

"Uh-huh. And this would be where?"

"Who knows?"

I glanced back at her again, ready to let her have it, but her expression said she was perfectly serious.

"What do you mean, 'who knows'? If this Vanished Place exists for the spooky, the bad and the ugly someone must know a way to send these demons there so they don't come back."

"I'm sure someone does, or has. I do not. Only the worst end up there."

"Seems to me Ficatier and Czcarabus qualify there."

"Maybe. But the point is moot because neither went to the Vanished Place."

For a museum curator she was just a fount of information on spooky things she shouldn't have known. I bet she wouldn't tell me but I asked anyway: "You know this how?"

"I can't answer that."

"Can't or won't?"

"Take your pick."

Bitch, bitch, bitch. "So you're telling me this Praetallious wants to bring back Angelique Ficatier and Czcarabus?"

"No."

"No?" My tone went up a couple notes. "What the hell do you mean, 'no'?"

"As in the opposite of yes."

That did it. "This isn't the time to be funny, even if for a friggin' moment anyone might have thought you were. I want answers now, Lansing. I think at this point Arlo and I deserve more from you than some kind of stupid word dance."

She didn't say anything for a couple more steps. The stairway wound down; we'd descended at least twenty feet so far.

"When Arlo Grimm confronted Ficatier and Czcarabus and stopped them from achieving their goal, a doorway opened. A doorway to the outer realms of Hell. There were...*things* lurking about that doorway, things that had found their way to it and were waiting for an opportunity..."

"To escape."

"Praetallious was one of them."

Oh, great. Just from the way she phrased it I knew Praetallious wasn't the only thing that had gotten loose. There were more nasties and even if Arly and I got out of this...

"What does he-it-whatever want?"

"Pestilence."

I stopped again, my stomach plunging. I looked back to her. "He's one of the Four frickin' Horsemen?"

"Oh, most certainly not. If he were he wouldn't be bothering with you. He's a minor demon but he can do a lot of damage."

Well, that was comforting...and oddly insulting. "So he's the one spreading this disease I heard about on the news?"

She nodded. "A variation of other plagues history has seen."

"Ring-a-ring of roses..." I said and she nodded again. "Can't give him points for originality, but why doesn't he just wipe out the whole town, then? Infect everyone in the state?"

"Evil doesn't work that way. It enjoys spreading fear, panic. That takes time, calculation. You'll find whoever was infected was part of a design, a plan to sow the most fear possible. He'll build on that."

I let out a nervous laugh. "So you're basically telling me fear is a dish best served in a crock pot?"

She didn't find that funny, I could tell.

"So if that's the case," I said, "it still doesn't explain why Praetallious didn't just kill Arly, or me, for that matter."

"He can..."

Whoops, didn't like the way she said that. I was almost under a notion we were protected because of that special thing she had mentioned.

"I thought you said—"

"Evil has a hierarchy. He can kill Arlo, but he was forbidden to do so."

Um, wait, she said Arlo. No mention of me. "And myself?" Did I really want the answer that one? Seemed like one of those damned if I did damned if I didn't things.

"You have the locket."

"That protects me?"

"To an extent but it is more than that."

"More. What?"

"I am not—"

"Allowed, yeah, yeah, I know. But he could have killed me before I got the locket, right? Special or not?"

"Possibly. Depends on what his superiors told him, though I suspect they would sacrifice you to get to Grimm...or if Praetallious could pass it off as an accident. You are of no use to them in bringing back something of Czcarabus' level, though returning Ficatier to this realm is a possibility. Even so, there are others they could use."

"That's totally comforting—Not!"

She almost laughed. One of the few times anything close to humor had shown on her face. "But you had other protection."

"Pat…" I whispered.

"She's trying to reach you."

"Then she's…dead?" My stomach headed south again and I swallowed at a knot of emotion suddenly lodged in my throat.

She shook her head. "I can't tell you that."

I wanted to grab her and shake the living crap right out her little Pixie ass. "Is there another choice?" My voice was getting shrill and I tried to calm myself.

"There are always choices."

"Goddammit, I wish for once you'd just come out with it."

"I'm sure you do. Things don't work that way."

Note to self: kick her ass if I get out of this in one piece. Kick it hard. And often.

"Where's Bob?" I asked, changing the subject before the urge to throw her down the stairs took over completely.

"He's claustrophobic. He wished to remain upstairs."

"Guess I would be too if my bones were in a box some place." I paused, then added, "So the locket…your monkey left it in my apartment. That means you told him to bring it to me."

"I did."

Wow. A straight answer for a change. Maybe there were some miracles left in this church. "How did *you* get it?"

"It appeared on my desk."

She wasn't lying this time, I could tell by her tone. "Why?"

"Someone wanted me to get it to you."

"Pat?"

"It belonged to her, did it not?"

"Ok, again—why? Why didn't she just leave it on *my* desk?"

She hesitated. "Because it was made for…"

"Made for?" I prodded. I got the sudden impression she had been about to say it had been made for her, but I didn't want to think about what that meant.

"We don't have much time…" she said, ignoring my question.

"That another one of your cryptic non-replies or are you just stating the obvious?"

Another glance back told me she was serious.

"I can't hold him off much longer," she said. "How's that for a non-reply?"

"Hold off who?"

"Praetallious."

"You're—what do you mean *you* can't hold him off?"

She didn't say anything further and I wasn't certain which irritated me more, her silence or her idiot non-answers.

We went down, the sound of my boots hitting the stone like a gunshot against each step. I started to sweat. I could feel it trickling down from my arm pits under my sweater. It might have been cool outside but in this stairway it was hot as...

Uh, great. Poor choice of almost word.

My heart banged, throbbing in my throat. It was as if I could feel something building, but couldn't see it. Like the air was thick with answers, yet all of them were invisible.

Another thirty feet down. The stairwell widened some and ended in a stone-walled room lined with torches.

I froze. It was as if time had suddenly stopped and the world had ended.

And I let out a cry.

THIRTY-THREE

The Discovery

"**A**rly!" I froze, my entire body shuddering with relief and horror at the same time.

The room was a large basement of some sort, walls dripping with moisture and coated with moss and some snaking branches that had wedged through cracks in the stone over time. Torches burned on the walls.

Arly was in the far corner, partially sitting, legs curled beneath his naked body, arms above his head, held to the wall by shackles. His head lifted when I let out my scream and my hands went to my open mouth. Bruises and scratches blemished his face and dried blood had caked beneath his swollen nose and at the corners of his inflamed lips. Praetallious may not have been allowed to kill him outright, but he'd sure spared no effort in beating him within and inch of his life.

"Chlo..." he mumbled, partially swollen-shut eyes trying to focus on me. "Chloe..."

I shook off my paralysis and ran to him, getting down beside him and throwing my arms around his neck. He groaned and I withdrew. My shaking hand went to his cheek and tears flooded my eyes, streamed down my face.

"Jesus, Arly," I said, voice quivering with relief. "I'm usually the one who ends up naked." I cranked my head back to Genie, who stood behind me now, peering down, little expression on her face. It was as if she'd expected to find him here. Something told me she had indeed expected just that, but it wasn't the time to try to pry an answer out of her.

"There's not much time," she said again and I didn't question her on it. I turned back to Arly. I had to get him to a hospital.

Getting to my feet, I grabbed one of the shackles, tried to pull it open like an idiot, but it wouldn't budge. They were locked about his wrists and I had no chance in hell of breaking them open.

I glanced around for a key, knowing damn well no demon would be stupid enough to leave one lying around. A small table stood next to Arly, one that held scraps of bread and a silver pitcher of brownish water. They had been keeping him alive, barely.

"Patricia..." Arly muttered. He was only half conscious, I realized.

"It's not her, Arly," I said, bending over him, kissing the top of his head. "It's just appearing as her."

"No...no, she...she tried to help me...came to me...but..."

"Shhhh, don't try to talk. We're going to get you out of here, somehow."

A laugh came then, like that of a little girl. Only this time it was deeper, laced with menace. I swung toward Lansing, who was looking towards the stone stairwell.

"He's coming..." she said, and I grabbed the silver pitcher from the table. I needed to find the key to these shackles, or at least get Sturdevant here with some kind of chain cutters before that demon showed up, but it looked like Lansing was right and time was just about up. Whatever she was doing to hold off Praetallious, if indeed she was doing anything, was being overpowered.

"Keep it away from him," I said to her and ran to the base of the stairs. I think I intended to brain the demon with the silver pitcher, for all the good it would likely do. Silver only worked against werewolves in movies; I doubted it would stop Mr. Pestilence.

I gazed up into the stairwell but saw nothing but flickering torchlight. A shudder ran through me and I wasn't sure whether to go up after it or wait until it came down. I had the feeling it wouldn't make much difference but my fingers tightened on the pitcher handle, my knuckles going white and my hand throbbing from gripping it too hard.

The laugh came again, a shuddery, distorted child's glee. "Frickin' demons," I whispered, trying to steel my nerve.

Behind me I heard a sudden double clank and spun, heart jumping into my throat. Both shackles had dropped against the wall and Arly's arms were free. Lansing was standing over him and the absurd jealous thought she was looking at my man naked jumped into my mind.

"How did—" I blurted.

She looked back to me and by her expression I knew a lie was already on its way out of her mouth. "They were loose," she said, turning back to Arly, and getting an arm beneath one of his own for support. I wondered if she were strong enough to lift him, tiny as she was.

I dropped the pitcher and ran to them. "No way those were loose. I pulled on them," I said, jamming my arm beneath Arly's other side and helping her hoist him to his feet.

"Does it matter?" she said, giving me an eyeful of shut the hell up.

"It will later, if we get out of this," I said, not letting her intimidate me. I braced Arly against the wall, while she held him there, his left arm draped over her pixie shoulders. I whipped off my sweater, thankful I'd bothered wearing a bra today, then tied it around his waist. Didn't need little Ms. Pixie Sticks getting more of an eyeful of his package than she had already. I'm not sure why I was jealous at a time like this but I was. I think it was a way to suppress the fear threatening to just crush any hope I had of getting Arly out of this church before that demon killed all of us.

I jammed my arm back beneath his left arm and we helped him towards the stairwell. He stumbled, nearly went down. It took all the strength I had to hold him up. By the time we reached the steps sweat was streaming down my face and from beneath my arms.

"Jesus, Arly, you're going on a diet," I muttered, mostly from nerves. I thought I heard him utter a thin chuckle, but my blood was pounding so hard in my ears I might have only imagined it.

Despite the fear threatening to overwhelm me, I don't think I have ever been so relieved in my life. Finding him, after damn near going out of my head with worry for more than a week now—finding him *alive*—it was more than I could have hoped for. But it wasn't going to matter if we didn't get him out of here soon. Either the demon or the combination of starvation, dehydration and the beating Praetallious had given him would finish him off and I damn well wasn't going to let that happen after coming this far. A few months ago, he'd moved Hell and earth to bring me back from the brink of death...I wasn't about to let him die on me now that the situation was reversed. I couldn't lose him.

The laugh echoed through the stairwell again when we reached the halfway point. It washed through me like a river of ice. Lansing made no sound and the expression on her face didn't change. She wasn't even sweating, though a bit of strain tightened her face. I still wanted to know how the hell she'd gotten those shackles off.

I was starting to gasp and my legs shook. I eyed the top of the well, about twenty feet distant, praying I wouldn't collapse before we reached it. I was thankful I spent a lot of time training my legs for dancing, but I wasn't used to holding up a 193-pound man.

"When we came in the door was locked from the inside..." I glanced at Lansing again, trying to take my mind off the quivering in my legs and burning in my lungs. "I saw no other way out down there."

She uttered some kind of laugh, like I was an idiot. "Demons don't need doors."

No, they just locked them from the inside then disappeared to wherever they disappeared to, I guess.

Arly was getting a little stronger. I think the circulation was coming back into his legs because he was suddenly supporting more of his own weight and that might have been the only thing that stopped my legs from buckling before we reached the top.

We came out into the church, and Bob was staring at us like we were late for a party or something.

We helped Arly down off the altar and into the aisle and I had the momentary notion we might actually get him out of the church and to my car before the demon showed up.

A laugh that echoed like thunder from the stone-walls killed that idea.

THIRTY-FOUR

Plaguing Me, Plaguing You

She was standing on the altar, the demon that looked like my sister. The Easter dress she wore was soiled, worn, faded, as if it had aged all those years since I'd last seen Pat wearing it. Her eyes shimmered with anti-light and something that could never be mistaken as belonging to a human being. Hunger. Infinite hunger. For fear, for death, for corruption.

"Chloe…" the thing whispered, holding out a hand. "Come to me, Chloe…don't take him from me."

"She's not your sister," Lansing said, urging me to keep moving towards the door with Arly.

Like I didn't already know that. "No kidding," I said, not bothering to hide my sarcasm. I couldn't have if I wanted to. I was scared enough to piss in my jeans so all my willpower was focused on not doing something that lame.

Lansing ignored the remark, something I'm pretty sure she got plenty of practice doing with those she didn't particularly like.

"Get him out of here," I said, keeping my gaze focused on the Little Miss Demonic.

"What?" Lansing said, for once an ounce of surprise in her tone.

I looked at her now, pulling every bit of courage I had left inside together. "I said, get him the hell out of here! Get him to the hospital. I left the keys in my car."

"Chloe…no," Arly whispered.

I wasn't particularly thrilled about leaving him in Lansing's lusty little hands, but I had no choice. This thing, Praetallious, wasn't going to get a second chance at him. I kissed him gently on his swollen lips, and my trembling hand went to his cheek.

"Go, Arly," was all I said. I knew he was too weak to resist or I would have had an argument on my hands. Lansing, however, might be another story.

"You can't beat him on your own," Pixie Sticks said, looking at me like I was an idiot child trying to pay for candy with Monopoly money.

"Can't I?" I said with a hell of a lot more confidence than I felt. She was probably right but at least if that thing killed me she'd never have the chance to rub it in. "I've got the locket. You said it would have protected Joan of Arc, right?"

A weird expression came into her eyes and I had no idea what it was, other than it looked incredibly sad.

"You won't get close enough to use it..." she said.

Thanks for your vote of faith, I wanted to say, but settled for, "Arly won't last much longer if you don't get him some medical help. He's special, you told me. And he was willing to give his life for mine a few months ago. I'm returning the favor."

She didn't spend time arguing with me, which was both a surprise and a welcomed relief. She shouldered his weight as I slipped out from beneath his other arm, then began leading him along the debris-strewn aisle. I could hear his whispered protests, but Lansing was a lot stronger than she looked; he was too weak to resist.

As I spun towards the thing, my gaze drilled Little Miss Demonic. "All right, you, it's time to kick some demon ass."

"No!" the demon girl said, the anti-light blazing more intensely in her eyes. "You can't take him. She needs him."

A not-so-nice two-word phrase almost came out of my mouth. I heard a nasty squeak come out of Bob, who was still perched on his pew top, so I think he covered it for me.

"I know what you are." A sudden skittering sound seemed to rise from everywhere about me and Bob began making ugly monkey noises. I caught glimpses of them from the corner of my eyes—rats, scurrying, their black eyes gleaming and maddened. They darted between pews and across the aisle. I shot a glance backward to see Lansing had gotten Arly to the door. On the wall sconce torches flared. Rats squealed.

I swung back to the demon.

"Stop it!" I could hardly move. I was frickin' scared out of my wits of rats but I kept telling myself it wasn't real. The thing was trying to scare me, make me lose focus. My hand went to the locket at my throat. The rats suddenly vanished and the locket felt warm, almost seemed to glow.

"I'm not afraid of you, Praetallious—whatever the hell you are." I was, but I was hoping this particular demon wasn't a mind reader.

Little Miss Demonic took a step forward, an odd smile on her lips. I could see patches of blackened green on her skin now; the sickly pallor to her flesh strengthened.

"She's coming back. You can't stop her." The thing's voice was a mix of Pat's and something else, something ageless, deep.

"Who, Ficatier?" I said, gripping the locket harder.

The girl nodded. "And after she returns, she'll summon the master, Czcarabus."

"Be another hundred years for that, bub, if I recall my demon history." I think I was just stalling because I didn't know what the hell to do next. I was all big talk when I got Lansing to take Arly out of here, but the time for talk was over and I was suddenly just a stripper without a clue how to combat Evil.

Bob was chittering behind me, and I got the idea he thought his noise-making was helping somehow but it was just getting on my already strung nerves.

"There are ways to hasten the ceremony. Ficatier has learnt them by this time."

"They have schools in Hell? Demon College?"

Little Miss Demonic took another step closer to the edge of the steps. The weird smile on her face widened, mocking me. She/it knew I was terrified. She could smell it on me.

"You lured Arly here, didn't you?" I said, trying to keep the shakiness out of my voice and suppress the fear running around like those rats in my stomach. "You gave him some clue to my sister to get him to this church."

The demon girl laughed and I wished to hell she would stop doing that.

"I provided the lead, but he would have eventually come here anyway. It was inevitable from the moment he offered to help you locate her."

I wasn't entirely certain if that meant this church actually did have something to do with my sister, or if the demon was simply taunting me.

"Is my sister alive?" I asked, steeling myself for the answer, but reminding myself demons weren't too damned likely to tell the truth anyway. They used your deepest desires and fears against you, remember? They lived on suffering, turmoil, dark emotions.

"But I *am* your sister, Chloe…" she said, taking the first step down.

Behind me Bob screeched and I couldn't blame him. A gasp came from my own lips.

Because what stood on the step was no longer a little girl…

THIRTY-FIVE

Sea of Hostility

She was me.

Or at least the spitting image of me as I had looked at about fifteen, except for the black-green patches and sickly pallor. The Easter dress had changed to jeans with torn knees and a loose T-shirt.

"You never tried to find me, Chloe," me said—I said—I mean...I don't know what I meant, because fear suddenly swirled with confusion. It wasn't me, was it? Me, but not me. My twin. Patricia. She would have looked just the way I did at that age, but the image was too close and I had the feeling the demon was pulling it out of me somehow—it was how I would have expected Pat to look had I known her then. The way I looked. Oh, yeah, confused was the word.

"If you were really Pat you would know I've spent years trying to find you." I tried to hold her/it/whatever's gaze but the anti-light glittering in its eyes seemed to be crawling around in my brain. I wanted to run, desperately, now that Arly was safe. But I couldn't, could I? I had to finish this, because Arly would never be safe if I didn't. Neither would I. These things that had escaped when Arly killed Ficatier...they were minor compared to what might come if we let them win, let them hurt others. People were dying by some plague this thing, this Praetallious, had set loose. I couldn't ignore that, either. My conscience told me it was a small battle in the scheme of things, but an important one.

"You let them take me, Chloe," the demon said. "You let them take me. You know what they did to me? The men in those homes I was sent to? They used me in ways that weren't human. They touched me and made me—"

"Stop it!" I yelled suddenly, a part of me worried that just such a thing might have happened to Pat. The thing knew it, was using it against me and I couldn't let it gain any more advantage than it had already. "Just shut up, Praetallious, or whoever the goddamn hell you are. You can't hurt me that way. I know I've done everything I could to try to find her. And I will keep doing it until I *do* find her."

The thing took another step down. As it did so it changed. Now, it appeared older, perhaps in its mid-twenties, still as I would have looked at that age, except that now the Pat-demon wore a nun's habit.

"You know I was here, now, don't you, Chloe?" the demon said. "You know how close I was to you all that time. But you were away, weren't you? You weren't searching for me. You were flaunting yourself in front of men, teasing them, making them *sin*."

A tremor of shock rattled through me and I couldn't stop it. How did the thing know I had been away from New Salem at that age? I had danced in circuits, mostly in Florida, for a time, before coming back to New Salem a few years ago. Had Pat come back to find me while I was gone?

A shudder of guilt replaced the shock. What if she had been here when I wasn't? What if I had missed—

No! It was just this thing working its way into my head, prying at my doubts and fears.

"I killed myself here, you know," the thing said, a vile smile spreading over its lips. "I hanged myself because I couldn't find you and because he wouldn't give up his vows for me."

Another bolt of shock. "What?" My voice trembled out, little more than a whisper. "Who? Who wouldn't give up his vows?"

The thing laughed, a more womanly sound, yet laced with sorrow and bitterness and cynicism.

"Father Lansing. I loved him, Chloe. But he didn't love me enough. So I hanged myself, from the rafters right up there." Her hand drifted up, index finger pointing to a spot high above the altar, at the beamed ceiling. And for reasons I couldn't have begun to understand, I wanted to believe the demon. I needed to believe it. What the hell—

"She's lying!" a voice snapped from behind me and my head twisted, the violence of the words breaking the spell that had been worming through me. Lansing stood there, halfway down the aisle. Anger and determination made her Pixie face a hell of a lot more intimidating that I had seen it be at any point up to this moment.

"Arly…" I whispered, then found my voice. "You're s'posed to be getting him to the hospital. Why the hell are you back here?"

Lansing's gaze remained on the demon, who suddenly backed up onto the altar, becoming the little demon girl again.

"Your friend, Detective Sturdevant, came." Lansing took a step forward. "He said you had left a message on his voice mail to meet you here. I had him get Arlo to the hospital. He'd get him there faster than I could, anyway. This thing isn't telling you the truth."

"Do you know the truth?" I asked her point blank, knowing I should have been focused on Praetallious but the need to know the answer to my sister's life and possibly death overwhelmed me.

"You are not allowed to interfere," said the demon, its voice now deeper, darker. "You have already done too much. Good is always screwing the rules."

Lansing let out some kind of laugh, a light, airy thing I would have attributed to nerves had it been anyone else. But I think she might have actually been mocking the demon. That seemed like a piss poor idea to me. My hand drifted to the locket, which felt warm again, and seemed to be almost glowing.

"I'll answer for that later," Lansing said, taking another step. "It's one of the drawbacks of freewill, isn't it? But you wouldn't know what that is…"

I got the sudden feeling Lansing and this thing somehow knew each other, had gone at it before in some way.

"A little fire, heretic?" The demon laughed again—God, I really hated that—and its hand snapped up. The flames in the wall sconces suddenly jittered, roared. One of them flared more than the rest, and a geyser of horizontal flame shot from it. The flame hit the aisle in front of Lansing, lashed in a waist-high circle about her, trapping her within.

For the first time I saw terror in Lansing's eyes. Terror and some sort of black memory.

THIRTY-SIX

Enter Stage Left, Praetallious

"**W**hat the hell is up with *that?*" I yelled, the last of my nerve deserting me. Now I was really scared and the urge to run grew almost overwhelming. Bob's incessant shrieking from the pew didn't help things much. I wanted to throw something at him.

Lansing looked spellbound with terror. A mean part of me briefly thought she deserved it for being such a Pixie Snit, but I was too frightened to hold onto the thought.

"You said Praetallious was pestilence—how the hell can he control fire?" He was a demon, I told myself, and that probably came with a bunch of evil abilities, though usually even the Big Horned Guy didn't dole out too many powers to one entity.

"He-he has help," Lansing stuttered, her misty-marble eyes glued to the flame, reflecting its jittering light.

"Who?" My head spun back around to see the Little Miss Demonic's eyes flashing with anti-light. But within that light I could see something, a dark teardrop of a reflection. And from within the teardrop, vague features, twists of ebony hair and mahogany flesh. And I knew—I *knew* who was aiding the demon.

"She's dead!" I yelled, looking back to Lansing. "She's in Hell, for chrissakes! This can't be happening!" Oh, yeah, it could. And was.

"He's channeling her," Lansing said, some of the composure coming back to her voice and to her face. "Part of her survived what Arlo Grimm did to her. That's why they brought Grimm here."

Ficatier. Angelique Ficatier. Dead witch walking…oh, crap, just crap. "So much for your blessed sword…" I murmured. Christ, if you can't cut off a witch's head and have her be vanquished to H-E-

Double-Toothpicks, what the hell good was an Inquisition sword, anyway?

Dammit, my mind was babbling. I had gotten so rattled I'd lost focus.

My head swung forward, my gaze locking back on the demon. I had faced Ficatier before, and she wasn't here now. Just a fraction of her was, or trying to be, and I would deal with that later—if there was a later. Praetallious was still the threat. If I didn't confront him nothing else would matter.

My hand went to the locket and I slipped it over my head. I took the stairs to the altar before I could even think about what I was doing. It was up to me this time. Arly was on his way to the hospital and Lansing was useless for some reason I couldn't fathom. Bob was, well, Bob was still being Bob and I'd slap his little monkey ass for it if I got out of this in one piece.

Little Miss Demonic suddenly belted out another one of her goddamn laughs and I shuddered as if it had been a chilled wind that rattled through my body. Sudden squealing and scampering filled the church and I almost froze with the sight of a hundred rats flowing from every nook and cranny, streaming across the altar. More flame leaped from sconces and shot outward, licking at the pews and fast-food debris. Bob let out a different kind of screech this time; I think his tail might have caught fire, but I didn't dare turn around and look.

Rats were overwhelming the place and flame was lashing everywhere. Little Miss Demonic was changing too, growing, her face mottling at first, then peeling back. Great flaps of flesh fell away to reveal some sort of greenish-gray hide beneath. Her hair dropped out and a moment later all that remained was a mottled skull with patches of green-gray cellophanelike tissue hanging in loose shreds. Its eyes still sparkled with anti-light but now Angelique's teardrop presence was gone. I had the feeling the demon was on its own. Whatever tenuous hold Ficatier had through him was only temporary, and something told me that was the one good thing I could grasp onto at this point.

The demon had become rounder, bigger, though it was still the size of an adolescent boy, maybe one like Pugsley from the *Addams Family*. It stared at me, or, more accurately, at the locket in my hand, which was suddenly not just glowing but downright hot.

"Jesus, can't any of you guys be freakin' good-looking?" I mumbled, trying to push away the terror running rampant through my mind.

This was a freakin' demon in front of me; the realization hit like a hammer on a thumb. Ficatier had at least looked human...this thing...this thing looked like a reject from one of those bad *Leprechaun* movies.

My legs started to shake and I got the immediate notion it wasn't simply because I was frightened. It was something the demon was doing.

A wave of heat washed over me, like I had suddenly developed a 103-degree temperature. I wasn't sure if it was the result of all the fire now lashing over the pews or something worse.

An instant later I knew it was something worse.

THIRTY-SEVEN

We All Fall Down

Something worse and something deadly. The thing was trying to stop me from getting close enough to use the locket and I knew damn well it probably could. I might be special in some way, like Arly, but Lansing had told me pretty much point blank I wasn't going to be special enough to beat this thing on my own. I was throwing away my life. I should have listened to her but it was too late. Praetallious wasn't going to let me get close enough to use the locket and the locket, protection for Joan of Arc to the contrary, wasn't going to be enough to stop the thing from affecting me and eventually killing me.

My bare arms were breaking out in sores, now. Patches of green-black flesh bubbled up and sweat streamed down my chest and from under my arms. Whatever plague the thing was spreading was devouring me.

I went to my knees, my legs suddenly too weak to hold me up. The demon laughed, a deep throaty thing, now, nothing like that of a little girl. I started to gasp, my mouth incredibly dry, my lips splitting. I could taste blood and something else, the flavor of rotting flesh that now filled the air. The flavor of disease, decay. The perfume of a demon.

Rats converged on me. They bit at my boots, my jeans. I let out a shriek and the locket dropped from my hand onto the altar. Where the locket had fallen the rats scurried back, leaving a clearing about it.

I have never felt such fear, even with that whole Ficatier and her Sisters of the Snake thing. I knew I was going to die and that was that. Lansing was helpless. Arly was on his way to the hospital but I knew somehow if I didn't destroy Praetallious that wouldn't matter, either.

Because Ficatier would return and this time…this time there would be no winning for him.

"Jesus…" I whispered, trying to summon whatever was left of my strength before the rats completely overwhelmed me. I reached out for the locket but the rats leaped at my hand and I jerked it back on pure reflex.

"You cannot win…" the demon grated in a voice that somehow foolishly reminded me of Jack Palance. "But you can join us…you can help me bring her back."

I gazed up at the thing, spite and defiance in my eyes. If I was going to die I was going to do it with my honor intact. "Never." My voice shook; my throat was parched, paining. "Never…"

"Chloe…don't give up…"

The voice came from beyond the demon and through blurring vision I thought I saw the wavering shape of a little girl.

"Pat…?" I whispered. "Pat, I can't do this…"

"Go away!" Praetallious shouted, flinging his hand back like some idiot monster in a B-movie. "You have interfered enough!"

The shape wavered, dissolved, and whatever help she might have given me went with it.

THIRTY-EIGHT

Like a Rat Out of Hell

The shrieking of the rats was tearing apart whatever was left of my nerves. Nausea coursed through my belly and I wanted to vomit. Pain lashed at every muscle, every fiber. Rats snapped at my legs and the exposed flesh of my sides. One hand hit the altar floor and they nipped at my fingers. Blood ran from small wounds. Pain radiated through my fingers and hands.

The locket...

Only an arm's length in front of me...and I could not get to it.

The heat from within me, from fever, and from without, from the flames, had grown intolerable. I was ready to hit the altar on my face and that would be the end. Rats and disease would consume me long before the flames sweeping through the church cremated what was left of my body.

From the corner of my eye something hurtled past me. Shrieking. Something furry with a singed tail and a mouth full of gleaming teeth and an attitude Cheetah would have been proud of. Bob was suddenly a flying monkey, well, more like a leaping monkey, but to my fevered vision he put any of those rejects from Oz to shame.

Bob landed smack on the demon's grotesque head, wrapping his arms about the monstrosity, his body covering the thing's glowing anti-lit eyes for a moment.

"Jesus..." I whispered, knowing the monkey had just given me the only chance I was going to get.

I had virtually nothing in the tank but I used the fumes. I forced myself up, flinging away rats and grabbing for the locket.

Getting it.

My hand closed around the locket and a sudden surge of strength washed through me. Rats vanished and along with them all the wounds they had made in my skin. The greenish boils disappeared and the fever drained from my body as if I had plunged into a cold stream. It was still intensely hot from the flames in the church, but in comparison that heat was nothing, at least for the instant.

It would be the end of me soon, however, if I didn't move now.

The demon was gyrating, its green-gray mottled hands grabbing at the monkey locked to its head. Bob shrieked as the thing tried to tear him free, as if its very touch was causing him pain.

I came to my feet, shaky, wobbling, and lunged, just as the demon hurled Bob. Bob flew again, this time ricocheting off a pew and landing in a furry heap on the aisle floor beyond the circle of flame that trapped Lansing.

I slammed into the demon, and it felt like grabbing a branding iron. I let out a shrill scream and almost jumped back out of reflex, but I knew I wouldn't get another chance.

I swung the locket up as the demon grabbed both sides of my ribs with blistering searing pain and tried to throw me back the way he had Bob. He achieved it, though I didn't fly quite as far. But he achieved it an instant too late. Because I had dropped the locket over his ugly bald head.

I hit hard, at the edge of the altar, pain splintering through my hip and side. The welts where his hands had grabbed my ribs faded. I pushed myself up, knowing even if the locket did anything to the demon the flames throughout the church were spreading faster now and would kill me just as surely as Praetallious. Smoke clouded the room, black and billowing. I started coughing, having trouble getting air.

From the altar, Praetallious was doing some sort of weird, shrieky gyrating dance. He could not pry off the locket, couldn't even touch the thing, in fact. He cast me a vile look, but it was brief, because he was already starting to…

Dissolve. That was the only word I had to put to what was happening. He was dissolving in great sloughing chunks. An arm dropped off and shattered into vanishing fragments as it hit the floor. Then the other arm followed, with the same results. His body just seemed to collapse into itself, crumbling to the altar. The locket melted, gold absorbing into the floor. Praetallious' head hit last, somehow still shrieking, but like the rest of his now vanquished form shattered to vanishing fragments.

"Yeah, yeah, I'm melting, just freakin' die already!" I yelled it more to steel my own nerves as I finally reached my feet than out of anything else. I could barely walk as I staggered down the altar steps. I couldn't deny the waves of relief coursing over me at seeing the damn thing going back to wherever it had come from, but I knew any victory would be short-lived if I didn't get out now.

My eyes met Lansing's. She was still paralyzed within the circle of flame.

"Get the hell out!" I yelled at her, waving my arm like an idiot.

"I can't—I can't!" Terror laced her voice. Something about the flames.

We all have our phobias, I guess.

Without even thinking about it, I hurled myself at her. Right through the first wall of flame, into her, and onward, both of us, through the backside of the blazing circle. This time I took a few burns and I was going to need a new bra, but we ended up on the floor together outside that circle of fire.

"We have to get out of here!" I yelled at her, getting back to my feet and offering her a hand up. Well, duh, but what else do you say in a situation like that?

Lansing nodded, some of her terror gone, but I could still see reflections of flame in her eyes and knew she was having a hard time keeping it together. We staggered down the aisle, reaching Bob, who lay unmoving on the floor. Lansing reached down, gently picked him up and cradled him in her arms.

"Is he…?" I asked, suddenly liking that monkey a whole lot better than I had in the beginning. If not for Bob…

"Dead? Yes, quite." She said it without much emotion, and that struck me strange. I was ready to cry over him and he wasn't my pet.

Then Bob opened his eyes and I think he might have smiled. It's hard to tell with a monkey because they always kinda look like they're smiling. Evilly.

"You said—"

Lansing uttered an uneasy chuckle as we reached the front doors.

"He's been dead for 600 years or thereabouts. He gets over it…"

Epilogue

I'd been awake most of the night and felt pretty much like hell. I spent most of my time at the hospital, half-dozing occasionally in the chair beside Arly's bed, but each time I even started to drift off I'd jerk awake with latent visions of what had happened in the church and a name on my lips: Angelique Ficatier.

Of course, before going to the hospital, I'd stopped off briefly at home to feed a grumbling Puddin' Head his dinner and get a new sweater. The Red Lagoon might like half-dressed strippers, but the hospital…not so much.

Arly was going to be in the hospital a day or two, getting his strength back. Nothing was broken and there appeared to be no internal bleeding or injuries, but he was dehydrated, half-starved and battered to a point that would take a week or two to recover from. I'd snuck him in the slice of pizza—black olive, heavy on the oregano—he'd bugged the hell out of me to get him for breakfast—ugh—and the nurse had given me sideways looks the rest of the morning. She hadn't seen it, but I knew she had smelled it and had pinned me as the likely suspect for smuggled snack foods.

I was running on caffeine and left-over adrenaline. My own wounds had all simply vanished with the destruction of Praetallious except for a few burns, and I had heard on the car radio all plague victims had mysteriously recovered. Doctors were at a loss to explain it. I was not.

I started my car and pulled out of the hospital parking lot. I was going to go home a get a little sleep before coming back later that evening, but first I had something I needed to take care of.

It was another gray day, charcoal underbellies of clouds threatening rain. I had half a notion to stop at the museum and try to get a few more answers out of Genie Lansing, but decided against it. She wouldn't tell me anything she didn't want me to know, anyway. I was certain, however, of one thing: she was no normal curator. There was something damned peculiar about her and she knew a hell of a lot more about what was going on, and what would be coming, in New Salem than she was telling.

Six-hundred-year-old-dead-monkey. *Pfft.* I still didn't want to believe that but a crawling suspicion told me she hadn't been joking. She wasn't really the joking type.

Later. After Arly got out of the hospital. I would let him handle her—though I'd keep a close eye. Couldn't be too careful with Pixie Sticks. The way she'd looked when she'd talked about him—yeah, right, I trusted her alone with my man.

A few minutes later I pulled into the parking lot at St. Luke's and killed the engine. Praetallious had said my sister hanged herself after what appeared to be an affair with a priest—Father Lansing. Was the demon lying? Most likely, but I needed to know for sure. And those with the name Lansing weren't particularly high on my list for trustworthiness, either.

I got out of the car, leaving my backpack on the seat. I went the church, tried the door, surprised to find it locked this time. I stared at it like an idiot for a minute—I think exhaustion was catching up to me and it wasn't just a blonde moment—then stepped away from the church and peered at the building behind it, which I pegged for the Rectory.

I walked around the church and went up onto a small porch, poked the door buzzer. Footsteps came from within, and I fully expected Father Lansing to answer, but it was an older woman who opened the door. She was heavyset, with graying hair and the look of a woman who had sucked one too many limes.

"May I help you?" Her tone seemed a bit bothered, and she gave me a look like I had sin written all over me. I got that look a lot.

"I was wondering if I could speak to Father Lansing for a moment."

Her brow knitted. "There's no Father Lansing here, dear."

Ack, I hated being called dear. "But I just talked to him yesterday, in the church."

"In the church?" The lines in her forehead deepened. "I sincerely doubt that, Miss. We keep the church locked. Vandals, you know."

"But I saw him there yesterday." I made my voice insistent but the fact was I had a gnawing feeling New Salem's supernatural had just crapped all over me again and I was looking like a first-class fool to this woman.

"You couldn't have seen Father Lansing, dear. Father Knox leads the flock here."

Leads the flock. Yeah, great. Who wrote their dialog, anyway? "Do you know where I might find Father Lansing, in that case?" I am pretty sure annoyance came into my tone. Her face pinched. Yup, I was right, and it bunched her Depends.

"Try the cemetery." I didn't care for the edge in her voice.

"Cemetery?"

"New Salem Cemetery. Father Lansing hanged himself, oh, must be going on ten years of thereabouts."

"Hanged himself?" Oh, yeah, if you're thinking a big rock plunged in my stomach…you nailed it.

"Over at St. Bosco's." She leaned in closer, her eyes sparkling with that weird sorta gleam gossips get when they snag the juiciest neighborhood news. "I hear tell he was having an affair with a young nun there."

I found myself back in my car a few moments later, a bit dazed, exhaustion really hitting me with the news of Father Lansing's death. So Praetallious had been only half-lying. It shouldn't have surprised me, but it did. That meant yesterday I had talked to…

A ghost? It was New Salem after all.

I supposed I should have felt a little relieved, too, because it wasn't my sister hanging from the rafters. But all I could think about was the fact that again, somehow, she seemed close enough to touch, yet at the same time so far away I would never learn the truth. Was she that nun at Bosco's? Was she alive? Dead? What about what Lansing had alluded to, about there being choices other than living or dead? I didn't have a clue what that meant but as I sat there, my forehead pressed to the steering wheel, both hands gripping it until my fingers ached, I suddenly remembered that line from the beginning of Arly's favorite TV show, *Dark Shadows*. Only in this case I could substitute my own name for that of Victoria Winters:

"My name is Chloe Everson…and my journey is just beginning…"

Oh, hell, yes, that just about said it all…

The Stripper Who Wouldn't Die...

Chloe Everson, Detective Sergeant Arlo Grimm's plucky stripper girlfriend, was never supposed to make it past the opening chapter of *Grimm*. She was conceived merely to serve as an informant for Arlo and meet her doom by sacrifice at the closing of "A Serious Error in Judgment", the short story that became *Grimm*'s opening chapter.

But a curious thing happened as that story built to its conclusion—Chloe didn't want to die. Not only had Arlo become attached to our headstrong exotic dancer, but the dancer herself had become attached to her fictional life!

Before long she took on an ever-growing dimension and capability. She became her own person, an equal to Arlo, perhaps even surpassing him in many ways. Before long, Chloe was clamoring to tell her own tales. And frankly I couldn't stop her.

Her adventures in New Salem grew into her weekly journal postings on *The Chloe Files* blogsite, which was supposed to be a one-time story arc designed to promote the *Grimm* novel. But again Chloe wasn't content with just one measly adventure. There was enough Evil in New Salem not only for Arlo Grimm but for further tales from *The Chloe Files*, the result of which is the first volume of the book you now hold in your hands.

Big things are coming in the months ahead for Miss Chloe Everson. The conclusion to *The Trouble with Flappers* (the first half of which was published as an Amazon Short), where Chloe meets a couple of murderous ghosts stuck in a 1920s party in a deserted mansion; werewolves and assorted ghoulies, and of course you know from this tale the New Salem Ripper is on the loose...

So join Chloe as she continues her journey into the macabre. And remember, there's Evil out there...waiting...

Don't forget to read the novel that started it all for our gal:

Grimm
by
Howard Hopkins

Available at fine online bookstores everywhere.

ABOUT THE AUTHOR

Howard Hopkins lives in a small Maine seacoast town and has written thirty westerns under his penname Lance Howard, the latest of which saw print in April, 2008, titled, *Blood Creek*. In addition, he's written six horror novels under his own name as well as comic book scripts, graphic novels, short stories and articles for various publications. He recently co-edited *The Avenger Chronicles* and adapted The Spider into graphic novel format for Moonstone Books. Visit his webpage at: http://www.howardhopkins.com. Also visit his Dark Bits blog at http://howardhopkins.blogspot.com.

And don't forget to check out Chloe's personal journal, The Chloe Files Online, at http://chloefiles.blogspot.com for the latest Chloe updates and story arcs.

Also by Howard Hopkins...

Grimm
The Nightmare Club #1: The Headless Paperboy
Night Demons
Dark Harbors
The Dark Riders
Pistolero

Lance Howard Westerns...

Blood on the Saddle
The Comanche's Ghost
Blood Pass
The West Witch
Wanted
Ghost-town Duel
The Gallows Ghost
The Widow Maker
Guns of the Past
Palomita
The Last Draw
The Deadly Doves
The Devil's Peacemaker
The West Wolf
The Phantom Marshall
Bandolero
Pirate Pass
The Silver-mine Spook
Ladigan
Vengeance Pass
Johnny Dead
Poison Pass
Ripper Pass
Nightmare Pass
Hell Pass
Haunted Pass
Desolation Pass
Blood Creek
The Devil's Rider

www.ingramcontent.com/pod-product-compliance
Lightning Source LLC
Chambersburg PA
CBHW052144170626
46812CB00004B/1582